# CHAP



James Daniels was seated at his desk, in his corner office on the top floor of the Fifth-Third Bank Center, thinking about the events of five days earlier. His office had two windows, each showing a spectacular view. The western window showed the Incline District of Cincinnati and, if he walked over to the window, he would look down onto the iconic Fountain Square which is the centerpiece of the downtown. Looking to the south, James could see the hills of Northern Kentucky and watch the barges slowly move north toward Pittsburgh or south toward Louisville.

On this day his mind was frozen on the incident of last week. He was seated at his desk when a secretary came running down the hall screaming, "Security just called and told me we are on lockdown as there is an active shooter in the lobby." James walked over to the window and looked down to see police cars parked in all directions and cops running toward the lobby of his building carrying tactical rifles. James walked over to the television in the office and saw that the local news was broadcasting live from outside the entrance. The reporter said that twelve people had been shot and two were dead. She also announced that the shooter had been killed by police.

James sat riveted to the news broadcast for over an hour until four police officers came down the hall telling everyone to evacuate the building. The cops escorted the people on the floor to a stairwell and walked them down to the lobby. The lobby was blocked off and they were

R. Barry Andrews

taken to a side door. The cops told them to go home for the day as the building was a crime scene and would be closed.

James walked to the parking garage and drove onto Interstate 71 in route to his home. He was in no hurry as there would be no one home at this hour of the day. His wife Karen would be at work and his son Dennis and daughter Kelly would be at school. The ride was spent thinking about the gravity of the incident and the status of his life as a whole. He had been unhappy at his job for several months and had thoughts of a career change. The car radio was on and he heard a commercial that Cincinnati was accepting applications for police officers. It might be just the career change he needed.

James pulled into the driveway of his home and opened the garage door electronically. He walked into the empty house and immediately removed his suit jacket and tie. As he walked into the kitchen, he saw his dog running toward him with her leash in her mouth. That was an indication she needed to go outside to do her business. James clicked the leash onto her collar and the two walked out the front door. The dog stopped in the front long enough to do her business and the two slowly walked down the sidewalk of the cul-de-sac. James saw a neighbor that he slightly knew on his riding mower his grass. Parked in his driveway was a shiny grey Dodge Charger with a blue light bar on top and markings on the door saying "OHIO STATE PATROL."

James and the dog stopped at the driveway of Dave Bristol and he waved until the man saw him. Dave turned off the mower and walked over to say hello. Although they were not friends, James said, "Dave, I have a question and need your advice. I am considering applying to be a cop in Cincinnati and was wondering if you could offer me any advice." A wry smile came to Bristol's face and he replied, "I am forty-four and we are about the same age. I have been a cop for nineteen years and I am not sure that I could pass the testing to become a cop if I had to do it now. The city will require you to run one and one-half miles in under twelve minutes, then do sit-ups, push-ups and pull-ups immediately after. You do not appear to be very athletic. That is not to say you are out of shape, but it can be tough for someone in their early twenties. If you are serious about making the cut, you will need to do several things relatively quickly. First, you will need to have one of your children drive while you run as far as you can. You will be able to ride back home in the car and it will tell you the distance you reached. Once you reach the mile and a half, you will need to work on cutting into the time that it takes. Next, you will need to build your strength. I have a full weight room in my basement and work out on Tuesday and Thursday evenings. You are welcome to work out with me."

James thanked him for the information and he and the dog went back home. He immediately got onto the Internet and filled out the online application. He sat in his recliner and turned on the news which was still broadcasting from his building. While watching, he tried to devise a way of telling his family about his decision.

James met his wife while they were both students at the University of Nevada Las Vegas. They decided to marry in their senior year and were planning the wedding when she got a job offer with Procter and Gamble Corporation in Cincinnati as a systems analyst. James' degree was in software development with a minor in finance, so he would have no issue finding a job anywhere in the country.

They were married in a church in Las Vegas and both of their families were able to attend. The two decided that their honeymoon would be the travel by auto from Nevada to Ohio. They planned numerous stops to take in the sites and enjoy the trip. When they arrived in Cincinnati, P&G had a short-term apartment for them and set them up with a realtor to find a home. They settled on a home in the City of Loveland, Ohio, a northeastern suburb, which actually sat in three different counties. That would be an important issue later. Their home was only a ten minute drive from where Karen's office and was close to an Interstate for wherever James was able to land a job. It did not take long for James to get hired as a developer for Fifth-Third Bancorp. His office would be in downtown Cincinnati, about a forty-minute drive each way.

They were in Cincinnati just under two years when Karen gave birth to twins, a boy they named Dennis and a girl they named Kelly. They loved their lives and felt blessed with what they had. James progressed in the company and would ultimately be given a membership to the Kenwood Country Club and paid parking in a close indoor facility. Karen was drawing a salary of just over eighty thousand dollars per year and, although James was making substantially less, they were not hurting for money.

***

The family had just finished dinner and the kids went off to their respective rooms to do homework. James made two drinks and motioned for Karen to follow him onto the back patio. There was a large back yard with mature trees and a lake that the builders of the subdivision had installed when the project was started. The residents kept the lake full of bass so that the residents could fish. When they were comfortably in lawn chairs, James said, "You know that I have been less than happy with my job. After the incident today at our building, I decided that I would like to be a Cincinnati cop." James waited to see the reaction on his wife's face, but there was none. He continued, "Any thoughts on me doing it?" Karen was quiet for a moment and then said, "I would have concerns about you being a police officer, but I would support your decision if that is what you really want. The salary would be significantly lower, but our house is paid off, our children have their college fund set up and our cars are all paid, so money is not an issue. What is the process you will have to go through to get hired?" James answered, "I will have to pass a written examination, then a physical agility test, psychological, medical physical, polygraph and an oral board. I have no idea what the last one entails." Karen asked, "Are you going to ask the twins for their input?" James replied, "Positively, it is a major life decision and they need to be a part of it." They relaxed and watched the sunset before going to bed.

The next day James went to a sporting goods store downtown during his lunch hour. He purchased a pair of expensive running shoes and a warmup outfit to wear for his runs. When his daughter got home, he had her drive the car as he ran and measure the distance he covered. James could see the quizzical look on her face and he told her simply, “I am not getting any younger and it is time for me to get my body into shape.” He was able to make just over half a mile and she drove him back to the house. It would take him almost three weeks to reach the one and one-half miles and then he started working on reducing the time it took to complete it. The first time he was on the clock, it took him just under fifteen minutes, so he had to cut three full minutes off the time. He took Dave up on his offer and would go to Dave’s house twice a week for weight training. The first evening Dave told him his goal would need to be bench pressing his body weight to build his muscles. James was not able to come close to the one hundred and ninety pounds that he carried and knew that he had much work to do. Within two weeks, he had significantly more energy and his general well-being was much improved.

***

James received an email telling him the date, time and location of the test. He arrived at the Cincinnati Convention Center thirty minutes before the test time. He sat and watched as people filed into the testing room and saw the majority of the people entering were young enough to be his children. He found that to be very intimidating.

The test itself was simple and he finished it with forty-five minutes to spare. He left the testing room and drove home, immediately changing into his running outfit and making the run in just over thirteen minutes. He had not told anyone at work that he was applying for a new job, as Dave told him the total testing process would take approximately six months. Six weeks later he received an email giving him the next phase in the process and that would be the run. He arrived at the Police Academy, which had formerly been the practice facility of the Cincinnati Bengals professional football team, where there were eleven other applicants. The applicants were paired into groups of four as there were four running lanes. James was in the second group which was sent off thirty seconds after the first group. James completed the run in eleven minutes and twenty seconds and was immediately directed to the center of the track. There was a police instructor waiting for him and he was told to do as many push-ups as he could in one minute. A short bottle was put underneath him to prevent his body from touching the ground. As soon as he completed that test, he was told to lay on his back and given the same instructions. The instructor held his legs down and he completed that phase. Lastly, he was told to do pull-ups on a bar set seven feet off the ground. At the completion of that test, James was told to relax for thirty minutes before the next phase of the agility testing would commence.

Dave had provided him information about the obstacle course. The instructor gave James a weighted police belt to simulate the weight of the police radio, gun and equipment. He would be required to run the course which had a simulated window to crawl through, a six foot high fence to jump or climb over, obstacles to run around. The course had to be completed in less than ninety seconds. When James was done, he was absolutely physically drained. The instructor smiled and told James, "Congratulations, you have passed the agility portion and you will be notified of the next stage." When James arrived home, he took a ten minute hot shower and took aspirin to relieve the pain.

Three weeks later his email notified him that he would be scheduled for the physical examination with the City's physician. His blood pressure, body mass and vital signs were taken and he was questioned about his medical history. His BMI was fifteen percent and the Doctor told him that was excellent given his age.

Two weeks later James was notified of the polygraph examination to be administered at the Criminal Investigation Section of the Police Department. James had fear that his use of marijuana in college might be an issue, but the operator told him it would not. The operator was about the same age as James and laughed when the two first met. The operator asked if James had ever taken a lie detector test and, when James said no, the polygraphist took the time to explain what would happen. He told James, "The actual lie detector test will take less than fifteen minutes. It will begin with an interview where I will ask you a specific set of questions about a number of topics. The fear people have is that there will be ambiguous questions and that it they will be subject to interpretations. The fact is that there will be no ambiguity in any of the questions you will be asked once we get to putting you on the machine. An example is that I will ask in the interview portion if you have ever stolen anything in your life. I will set a value of say five dollars and continue to raise the dollar amount until you can safely answer no. Other questions we talk about in the interview will have, 'Besides what we have talked about' in front of the question. I will write your answers in the interview down and all of the information will be sent to the recruiting unit for their evaluation." The interview portion took over an hour and James was only hooked to the machine for ten minutes.

He received another email scheduling him for the psychological evaluation. The message told him that this would be a two-day test with Dr. James Don, the contracted psychologist for the city. James did a google search on the Doctor and learned that Dr. Don had been the City's psychologist for over twenty-five years and specialized in dealing with police officers.

The first phase of the testing was a five hundred and eighty question multiple choice test. James quickly noticed that the questions were repeated with minor changes. James thought this was an honesty issue to see if the person taking the test was being honest in their answers. The second day was actually meeting with Dr. Don. James was taken to a small room with comfortable chairs. Dr. Don came into the room with a smile on his face and introduced himself, then asked, "What made you decide to become a police officer at your age?" James thought for a moment and answered, "I was tired of my nine to five life and wanted something more challenging. I was in my office on the top floor of the Fifth-Third Center when the mass shooting occurred and saw cops running toward, not away from, the lobby of the building." Dr. Don had James relate his life experiences and asked how his family felt about his becoming a police officer. James said, "I sat down with my wife first and then talked to my two children and they are supportive of my choice. I also talked to a neighbor who has nineteen years with the Ohio State Patrol who laid out expectations and experiences." The interview lasted a little short of one hour and Dr. Don wished James well.

James left wondering how many of the five hundred who took the written examination were still in the running and how many would actually get hired. Two weeks passed and James had not heard anything. When he spoke to Dave, he was relieved to hear that he would have received notification if he had been removed from the eligibility list. Two more weeks had passed when he received an email from the city that he was scheduled for the Oral Board, which is the final stage in the hiring process.

The final interview was held at the Police Administration Office on the second floor of District One headquarters. When he entered the room, there were three uniformed police officers seated at a table and a single chair in the center of the room. The three Captains were right around the same age as James and the first question from one of the Captain's was, "Aren't you a little old for this type of career change?" James smiled meekly and answered, "I thought long and hard about that exact question. I sought advice from my neighbor who has been with Ohio Highway Patrol for nineteen years. He told me that he was not sure that he could pass the entrance tests if he had to take them now, and then helped me prepare for the rigors of the testing process." Another Captain asked, "What is your goal with this agency should you get hired?" James took a minute and answered, "My goal is a career that challenges me every day. I have no long-term goals as I have been a supervisor of over one hundred people for the past ten years. Money is not a major consideration as I am financially set for my family's needs." After the questioning was completed, one Captain asked, "Do you have any questions for us?" James said, "Only one, how many people will actually be hired?" One Captain answered. "forty-five will be invited to the next recruit class. We wish you well and you will be notified within the next four weeks." James left the interview feeling comfortable that he had put his best foot forward.

The anticipation increased as the weeks passed. After not hearing any news for four weeks James called the Civil Service Commission and was told that the Police Department had not sent them the list of people hired. James was seated at his desk when his cell phone dinged that he had an email. The email said:

*"This is to advise you that you are being offered conditional employment with the City of Cincinnati. This offer is contingent on successful completion of your background investigation.:*

James immediately called Karen at work and read her the email, then smiled as she said, "woo hoo."

A woman called him at work the following day and identified herself as an investigator with the Recruiting Unit of the Cincinnati Police Department. She wanted to set a time and date for a home visit when the whole family would be present. She arrived and wanted input from all the family members as to whether they supported the decision to be a police officer. Two days later James received a call from his parents telling him a cop from Cincinnati had come to their house in Las Vegas to talk to them about him becoming a Cincinnati Police Officer and then talked to all of their neighbors about his childhood.

The investigator called him to ask for permission to talk to his current employer. She told him that she waited until her investigation was almost complete to avoid any adverse consequences in his current employment and that her final report would be sent to the Police Chief within days.

Two days later James received a call from the investigator telling him that an issue had come up that needed to be resolved. She told him, "The City has a residence requirement that all employees must live within Hamilton County. The City of Loveland sits in three different counties and we need to verify you are within Hamilton County. The proof is where you pay your property taxes, so we need a copy of your last tax payment." James answered, "My wife pays all of the bills, so I will not be able to provide that until tomorrow." He sent a fax copy of the payment and heard no more.

James received an email from Civil Service telling him that he would be starting the Cincinnati Police Academy in three weeks and that his probation period would begin on his first day and would be for a one-year period.

James wrote his letter of resignation to his employer thanking them for the trust they had placed in him and called a staff meeting of his staff to tell everyone. They held a going away party on his last day with many dressing in police uniform costumes.

His new life was beginning.

## CHAPTER TWO

James was unsure what to wear for his first day of his new job so he wore a short sleeve shirt with tie and dress slacks. When he walked into the Academy at seven thirty, the secretary asked for proof of identification before allowing him past her. She directed him to a room where there was coffee, juice and danish for all of the recruits. James found a table and watched as the class congregated, most of them being young enough to be his children. A few of the recruits asked him questions thinking he would be one of their instructors. A man walked into the room a few minutes before eight wearing a tee shirt with the logo of the Cincinnati Police and the word "Instructor" under the logo. He told them it was time to get started and led them to the classroom. As James passed through the entrance, he saw a sign hanging above that said, "The finest police officers in this country pass under this sign."

There were nameplates on all of the desks in the classroom and James was happy to see that he was not in the front row. In the basket under the chair were five five-inch thick empty binders with the Cincinnati Police logo on the outside of each. Neatly folded were five gray tee shirts with the recruit's name on the back and five pairs of gray slacks for each recruit. Also included were two pairs of shorts.

A uniformed police officer walked into the room and the staff instructor yelled "ATTENTION!" The room of recruits all got rigid until the police officer said, "At ease." He said,

"My name is Lieutenant Charles Sanders and I am the Commander of the Police Training Unit. I would like to welcome each of you to the one hundred and second police recruit class. Each of you earned your way here and our job is to help you be successful in your police career. As this class progresses, some of you will decide that this is not the career you want. I would like to announce that the Rocko School of Typewriter Repair is now accepting applications and some of you should seriously consider enrolling. The door to this room locks at eight o'clock. If you are not in the room, you will sit in the hallway until the next hour and that will not happen often. Our staff will help you in any way that we can because we want you to be successful. In the history of this Police Department, only two Police Chiefs did not graduate from this academy. We train leaders. You will be required to pass two written examinations in order to graduate. One will come from the State and we administer one of our own. If you have any questions or issues, feel free to come to my office. Best wishes in this new adventure. Your daily schedule is on your desks. You will fill all five of those binders before the end of the class and the organization of those binders will be pass/fail. They will be inspected regularly by instructors and all notes in them are required to be typewritten."

The instructor told the class that every time the door to the hallway opened that they were to immediately jump from their seats and stand at attention until told to sit. They were informed that it did not matter whether the person coming into the room was the Police Chief or the Custodian. They were to show respect to everyone entering the classroom.

The instructor asked each of the students to tell the class why they chose this career. When it was his turn, James told the class, "I was seated in my office on the top floor of the Fifth-Third Center on the morning of the mass shooting. From my window, I looked down on Fountain Square and saw police officers running toward the lobby of my building knowing there was someone with a gun shooting people. It was at that moment I knew that this was what I wanted to do the rest of my working life."

James looked around the room and counted that the class was made up of twelve white males, twelve females, ten black males, and four Asians. He thought about the original written examination where over fifty percent of the attendees were white males.

The recruits were taken to a locker room to change into their uniform and prepare for the rest of the day.

Their morning was spent completing paperwork for their salary and benefits, pension, calisthenics and the daily run. They were told they could eat lunch in the breakroom or leave the facility and they would have one hour of free time. James did not bring his lunch and several of the group decided to go to Frisch's Restaurant to eat. The students were curious about the decision process James had in deciding to become a cop at his age.

Day two began the classroom portion of the police academy. For the next three weeks, James would be totally engrossed in notetaking, much more than he ever did in college. The recruits were administered written tests at the end of each week covering the things they had been taught. James learned that the State of Ohio Peace Officer Training Commission gave the questions and the answers to their tests, calling them Student Performance Objectives (SPO's). The recruits would receive the question and a choice of several answers and, when the actual test was given, only some of the correct choices would appear. The class had already lost two of the recruits and there were rumors that a few more were in jeopardy.

James had taken over the kitchen table and used it as his study point after the table was cleared from dinner. He overslept one morning and had to rush to get out the door for class. He was driving on Interstate 275 when he looked into the mirror and saw blue and red lights flashing behind him. He quickly pulled over and placed both hands out of the driver's side window with his driver's license and insurance card in his hand. He was awaiting the officer to approach when he heard tapping on the passenger side window. James rolled the window down and the deputy sheriff looked inside, immediately seeing the blue binder with the Cincinnati Police logo. The deputy asked, "What is that?" James smiled meekly and answered, "I am in the Cincinnati Police Academy and I would really appreciate if you could write the ticket quickly so that I am not late. The deputy smiled and handed back the driver's license saying, "I would hate for you to be late. Enjoy your day." With that, the deputy turned and walked back to his cruiser.

Week Five sent the class to the Firing Range which was located in the north end of Cincinnati outside of the city limits. The first two days were in the classroom learning about the operation and handling of a semi-automatic handgun. The students were trained in removing the weapon from a high security holster which was designed to thwart others from being able to remove it. They were taught drills to fix malfunctions common with semi-auto handguns that render them useless until cleared. One instructor told the class that the weapon became a six hundred dollar hammer until whatever the malfunction was got cleared.

When they were taken out onto the firing range, the instructors checked with each recruit to determine their level of expertise. When James was asked, he told the instructor that he had never touched a firearm in his life. The instructor got a wry smile on his face and told James that it was the best of all worlds because he did not have any bad habits that needed to be broken. James was moved to the end of the line of recruits and has his own instructor to get him started. He was told to load a magazine of ammunition into the weapon and then pull the slide back to load a round into the chamber. The instructor told him to smoothly pull the trigger back until the weapon fired. After the first six shots were fired, James was visibly shaking as he looked at the target paper with no holes in it. The instructor softly told him that there was nothing unusual about that as James has what is called 'Pre-Ignition Push' or PIP. That occurs when the shooter is anticipating the bullet being fired and jerks at the last second causing the bullet to shoot into the ground. After a second try, the target still had no holes so the instructor stood directly behind James and held the weapon with James. He placed his finger over James' finger in the trigger and smoothly pushed the trigger until the bullet fired.  The instructor felt him flinch as the round came out and hit the center of the paper target. He continued to improve and was moved back in with the rest of the recruits. He went home and told his wife that this was not nearly as easy as it looks on television.

The last day of handgun training required passing the proficiency test that the State of Ohio mandated. All but three of the recruits passed the shooting test without problems. The last three were told that they would be given one last attempt to complete the test. Failure would end their employment with the Cincinnati Police. James learned something he had never experienced in his years in the business world. The recruits all stayed and served as cheerleaders for each of the three who needed to re-test. The first, a female officer got three practice runs through the testing, but failed the actual test. She was escorted from the range never to be heard from again. The second, a male, made it through by a single point and received hugs and high-fives from the other recruits. When it was time for the last of the recruits to step up to the range, he withdrew his firearm and handed it to the instructor, saying simply, "I am done. This is not the career for me." With that, he turned and walked off the range to find another career.

The next phase of the training was firing a Remington twelve-gauge pump shotgun. Prior to actually firing the weapon, the recruits were given specific instructions on proper loading, safety and firing procedures. After practicing with inert rounds in the classroom, the recruits were taken out to the range to shoot live ammunition. The first set of recruits got on the firing line and loaded their weapon. When the command was given to fire, one of the recruits suffered a separated shoulder because he ignored the proper firing procedures. A female suffered a broken jaw when the recoil of the shotgun smacked the right side of her face. Neither ever returned to the class after being transported to the hospital for treatment. When James went home that night, his wife had to apply liniment to his right shoulder to relieve the pain.

Upon completion of this training, the students were introduced to the Taser©, a less than lethal weapon. Actually called an Electro Magnetic Dysfunction Device, Taser is a manufacturer name, the device causes the involuntary dysfunction of the muscles by sending ninety thousand volts into the body. It is fired into the body from a trigger operated plastic weapon and pressure-coiled wire. The two prongs attach to the body creating a circuit, causing the muscles to malfunction, which temporarily disables the suspect. It is not classed as a firearm because it is not propelled by an explosion. The recruits stood in a single line with the students on the ends each holding one prong. When the trigger was activated, the voltage went through each of the students with the ones in the middle taking the brunt of the voltage. There were a lot of, "FUCK, THAT HURT" heard from the recruits. The point of the exercise was to demonstrate to the students the impact the weapon has when deployed.

The last phase of this training was the use of the bean bag shotgun, which fires a cloth bag to temporarily disable an offender who is non-compliant.

The students returned to the Police Academy for self-defense training.  This is to learn to handle physical confrontations with non-compliant individuals. Defensive Tactics is a stand-alone training per the State guidelines. If a student fails this phase, they are removed from the overall program and unemployed.

The recruits were paired to practice and learn from each other. James was paired with a twenty-three year old recruit who played linebacker for the University of Cincinnati football team. When the pairing was announced James asked, "Do you want to see me hurt that badly?" His partner said, "You want me to hurt a man old enough to be my father?" The instructor demonstrated moves designed to get a person to the ground inconsequential of their physical size.

The instructor, who stood five feet nine inches tall, chose a six-foot four inch two hundred forty pound student to demonstrate. They were in the center of a wrestling mat when the instructor told the recruit to attack him. The student lunged and landed flat on the mat in under two seconds.  The instructor walked over to the big man lying on the mat and said, "You let the OLD guy put you there, you need to be ashamed. You will never live that down." James extended his hand to help the recruit get to his feet while the rest of the class hooted and hollered. The big recruit immediately picked James up off the ground and dropped him to the mat saying, "Now we are even." The big guy extended his hand to help James back to his feet. The class was definitely bonding.

The next three weeks were all in the classroom and James was filling binders quickly. He would go home each evening and type the day's notes and specifically list the Student Performance Objectives that they had been given to provide a study manual for the final examination.

As they were approaching the end of the week, the recruits were told they would be out on the streets for the following two weeks to watch and learn the realities of police work. James was assigned to the evening shift in District Five which covered the area of the University of Cincinnati campus.

***

James reported to District Five for the six pm to four am shift. His trainer had twenty-two years experience and was low key. Don Busch shook his hand and told him, "Just relax and learn. You don't have anything to prove to me. We will do our job and go home each night." They were assigned to the north end of the District. They had just reached their beat when an All County Broadcast put out an officer needs assistance just outside the city limits in Springfield Township. Busch jumped on the gas pedal as James initiated the lights and siren. They arrived to find the Springfield Township cruiser, but no officer to be found. Additional cruisers from multiple jurisdictions were arriving by the minute and the units on the same police frequency were asking for information on where the officer was. It took a minute or two for someone to find the officer who was bleeding from the face. He told officers that the suspect grabbed the officer's flashlight and hit him in the head. Busch called Communications to get a canine unit to the scene and was told that one was in route. The Springfield Township canine arrived first and it only took a few minutes for the dog to locate the suspect who tried to fight the one hundred pound canine named Banacek. The dog bit the suspect several times, leaving him bleeding profusely from the legs and arms. Officers stood and watched until the handler called off the dog and then handcuffed the suspect who still had some fight left in him. Busch looked at James and said, "Our services are no longer required, we can go back to our beat."

The two were driving north on Hamilton Avenue following a grey Mercedes that was having issues staying in its lane. James initiated the lights and the Mercedes accelerated and the chase was on. They stayed with the vehicle as it left the city entering the City of North College Hill. James kept communications updated as to their location and North College Hill Police joined the pursuit. They cleared North College Hill and entered the City of Mount Healthy who had a roadblock set up on the four lane road. The Mercedes crashed into two police cars bringing it to a stop. Officers rushed the vehicle which was being driven by a teenage female who was clearly intoxicated. All three jurisdictions decided to file charges against the girl, the most serious coming from Mount Healthy Police who lost two police cars.

The shift came to a close with Busch telling James, "We done good. We are going home."

The second day the two started the shift by picking up coffee at a White Castle restaurant. They were drinking the coffee when they were dispatched to an address on

Cedar Avenue in College Hill to do a welfare check on the resident. They parked in front of the house and, as they approached the porch, the stench was palatable. Busch used his ASP expandable baton to bang on the front door, but no one answered. The two cops walked around the house searching for an open door or window without success. When they got back around to the front Busch said, "We do not have a warrant to kick in the door, but we have a suspicion that something is wrong. In this type of situation, you want to call for a boss and let them make the decision. Busch called Communications and requested a supervisor respond to the home. A female Lieutenant arrived and Busch explained what they had. She authorized them to force entry into the house. Busch kicked the door at the handle, but it took three tries until the door flew open. The stench came out of the front door with such magnitude that James felt like he was about to vomit. The three walked into the house and searched until they found a male, who looked to be in his sixties, dead in a chair. It appeared that he had been dead for days, maybe weeks, as there were maggots on his face. The three backed out of the house and the Lieutenant called Communications to have Homicide investigators and the Hamilton County Coroner's Office respond. She ordered them to secure the scene until they were released by the Homicide dicks. Busch told James to stay at the door and went back to the cruiser. He returned moments later with a jar of Vicks Vape-O-Rub. Busch told James to rub it on his upper lip. When James did it, the smell went away and all he could smell was the menthol from the salve. A covered pick-up truck arrived about forty minutes later and two males wearing Hamilton County Jail coveralls brought out a black body bag and waited for the arrival of the detectives. Two detectives arrived about ten minutes later and used the same salve to enter the house. After another fifteen minutes they told the volunteer inmates to go into the house and remove the body. It took about thirty minutes for the body to be packed into the body bag and placed into the truck to be transported to the Coroner's Lab. The detectives asked James if he had touched anything inside the house and looked relieved when James said that he had not. The Cincinnati Police Forensic van pulled up and three crime scene specialists unloaded gear from the van and went into the house. Neighbors were now coming out of their homes to see what was happening and Busch went back to the cruiser to retrieve yellow crime scene tape to close off the area. Two hours later, the detectives told the two cops that it was okay to leave. When they got into the cruiser, Busch asked James if he was ready for lunch. James was feeling queasy, but said he was and they went to a Frisch's Restaurant to eat.

When the shift was over, James drove home, entering his house through the basement. He stripped down to his underwear and threw the uniform in the washer to get rid of the smell. James decided that he needed to install a shower in the basement so that he would not have to take the smells of the job through the house.

When the two cops got into the cruiser to start their shift Busch quipped, "Two days down and you have already seen a lot. This job is hours of boredom and instant terror. You have seen a lot and will see a lot more each day. Don't let it get to you, it is just a job. Don't make the mistake of taking what you have seen home with you. Concentrate on your family when you are home and your job when you are here. What you learn in the Police Academy is important and necessary, but how you apply what you learn is determined out here on the street."

At the end of the two weeks working the streets Busch told James, "You will clearly do well in this organization. You have a disposition that will de-escalate difficult situations and teach young cops the ropes to be successful. I wish you the best as your career progresses."

The recruits reported back to the Police Academy to finish their training. Standing at the podium as they sat down was the Commander of the Police Training Unit who said, "Ladies and gentlemen, you have had the opportunity to put into practice the things that you have learned here and found out you have a lot more to learn. The fact is that, no matter how many years you put in here, you will never stop learning. We could spend our whole lives in the classroom training and never be prepared to provide our citizens the service that they demand, but there would never be cops on the streets. You will learn from doing and learn from watching. The rules of this game continuously change and you need to be able to adapt to those changes if you want to be successful. You will hear cops tell you that your employment is protected and they are correct. What they fail to tell you is that the Administration of this department are not protected and the politicians can replace them with people who do not care about protecting you. In fact, the politicians can come in and dissolve this agency and you no longer have protection. We serve at the pleasure of the citizens of Cincinnati."

The majority of the remainder of the training program was in the classroom. The exception was the driving portion where the recruits actually got to experience emergency driving techniques hands-on.

As the recruits were preparing for the State examination, James got a group together to study together. They would meet at each other's home or apartment and each would bring a question which might be asked on the real test. When test time came, the group was well-prepared and eased through the two hundred question multiple choice test.

The graduates were awarded their police badges at a ceremony at Convention Center. It was attended by the Police Chief, all of the Command Staff and the Mayor and City Council members. The recruits all had their families in attendance and it was a celebratory event. The recruits reserved the Westin Hotel downtown for a party that evening and James made a reservation to stay the night. There was an open bar and a disc jockey and the dancing went on until late into the evening. The recruits also got their initial assignments to start their career.

James and Karen decided to take a family trip at the end of his first week of work. They decided to go camping in northern Ohio in an Amish community where there would be no distractions and allow everyone to just relax. They decided to allow Dennis to bring his girlfriend and Kelly would bring her boyfriend.

# CHAPTER THREE

James got his assignment to report to District One working the six to four first shift on Monday. His Field Training Officer would be Police Specialist Doyle Frock, a twenty-six year old with just under five years under his belt.

James parked in the back lot and had to yell to get a cop entering the rear entrance because he did not have the required code to open the door. The Sargent introduced Frock and the two sat through the roll call of the events from the earlier shifts. They were assigned to the Fountain Square area running beat 1104. They were just loading the cruiser when they were dispatched to Fifth and Walnut for a crash involving a Metro bus. Frock told James to issue the bus driver a citation for Failing to drive in marked lanes. Frock read the citation to make sure it was correct before having James get the driver to sign the ticket. The driver said, "You are giving me the ticket because I am black." James replied, "The other driver is black too." Then the driver said, "You are giving me the ticket because I am male." James laughed and replied. "The other driver is male as well." Then the driver said, "I will get suspended because you wrote this fucking ticket." James thought about a response and just turned and walked away.

When they returned to the cruiser James asked, "I need a favor. I would like to stop at Fifth-Third Center to say hello to my former employees." Frock smiled and said, "It is in our beat, I have no problem with that." They parked on Vine Street and walked up to the main entrance of the

Center. They approached a guard sitting at a desk and James said, “Hello Henry.” The guard got a puzzled look on his face and there was nothing said for about one minute. The guard looked hard into James’ face and said, “Mr. Daniels?” James laughed and said, “You got me, it is me. I was hoping to go to the top floor and say hello to my former employees.” The guard smiled and answered, “Cincinnati POlice go wherever they want.” With that the two cops went to the elevator and rode to the top floor. When they got off the elevator, the secretary looked shocked to see two uniformed cops on the floor. It took a minute but her face lit up and she yelled, “MISTER DANIELS!” James blushed and replied, “It’s not Mister anymore, it’s just James.” The secretary ran down the hallway yelling for the employees to come out and the men shook his hand and the women all hugged him. The visit only lasted a couple of minutes and the two cops went back to work.

The rest of the day ran smoothly. The two got the chance to do a lot of talking in the car. Frock told James that he got the strange recruit assignments. His last recruit was formerly a Police Chief of a small municipality and had fifteen years of experience as a cop. He confided that having a recruit almost his father’s age presented an intimidating adventure, but this could be an opportunity for both to learn and get better. Frock would provide the police skills and James could provide the people skills he developed over years of being a manager in a non-police environment. James felt really good about his FTO.

Day two had the pair assigned to the West End which Frock called the 'hood.' It is a low-income area with a high crime rate and drug problems. Frock drove around explaining the areas which presented the highest crime rates in the city.

Frock told James that he had a court case scheduled for trial and it would provide an opportunity to watch the system from an observer point of view. The two walked into the Hamilton County Courthouse twenty minutes before the case was scheduled to start. Frock showed James where the snack shop was located and the two got coffee to take upstairs. They were standing in the hallway chatting when James saw a red blinking light above a courtroom door. When he asked Frock about the light, Frock dropped his coffee and said, "That is a Judge's panic alarm." The two ran into the courtroom where a full-scale brawl was happening. A Court bailiff was wrestling with a large frame African-American male and two sheriff's deputies were attempting to subdue another man. People were fighting in all sections of the room and the female Judge was bleeding from being struck in the head with an unknown object. James jumped in to help the bailiff who was struggling to control the suspect. James deployed his Taser and the male screamed in pain, but complied. Cops from different agencies came running into the courtroom and, after about ten minutes, multiple people were in handcuffs. He would be told later that a jury had just convicted a man of sexually assaulting an eight year old girl when her father leaped over the railing and the fight was on. Both families then squared off and the battle royale was on. Luckily a news crew was in the room and caught the whole thing on camera. James was glad that this would be a mess for the Sheriff's Department to investigate. When they got back to their cruiser, Frock quipped, "Well, that was a learning experience for you. Just not quite what I wanted you to learn."

At the end of his first week in the FTO program, the two sat in the roll call room going over his review. Frock pushed the completed form for James to sign and told him, "We were pretty lucky this week. I try to move slowly with my recruits to allow them time to get comfortable with the job. You did not get the chance to do a lot of things and that was intentional. You will do more and more as the weeks progress, and the reviews will get more and more harsh. I want you to be the best that you can be."

***

James woke up to an empty house on Friday morning, something that he was not used to. The kids were at school and his wife was at work. He made coffee and sat down to read the rag morning newspaper. When he actually felt awake, he went out to the garage to load the trailer for the weekend family trip to Amish country. He loaded the tent which would sleep eight people, three double sleeping bags, a propane grill, and a large heater as it would be cold in northern Ohio. Both his son and his daughter would be bringing their significant other along with them. He had the trailer set up to connect to Karen's Lexus and waited for everyone to get home.

The drive would be just over three hours to Wooster, Ohio and Karen came home early from work. They left as soon as the kids arrived home from school. James was driving north on Interstate 71 north of Columbus, Ohio when he saw blue lights flashing behind him. He immediately pulled over and rolled the passenger window down awaiting the trooper. When the trooper approached, James opened his wallet to withdraw his driver's license and insurance card, also exposing his police badge. James told the trooper, "I had the cruise control set at sixty-five, so why are you stopping me?" The trooper looked at the wallet and replied, "The taillight on your trailer is not functioning, get it repaired." James smiled and said, "I will get it fixed as soon as we reach Wooster." With that, the trooper walked back to his cruiser without ever looking at his driver's license.

When the group arrived in Wooster, James pulled into the parking lot of Der Dutchman, an authentic Amish restaurant featuring comfort food. After they ate, they drove to the campsite and then to their assigned space. The males set up the tent while the girls emptied the other items from the trailer. When the tent was up, the boys went searching for wood for the firepit and the group had a roaring fire soon after. They roasted marshmallows and enjoyed the clear evening before retiring to the tent for the night. The tent had a zipper to completely close it off from the cold air and the heater was set in the center of the tent to push warm air in a 360-degree direction.

When they woke up Saturday morning, the girls fired up the propane grill while the boys trekked to the General

Store for supplies. The bathrooms were more than one hundred yards from their campsite and there was frost on the windows of the Lexus. After the girls made bacon, eggs and home-fried potatoes, they all cleaned up the mess they had made.

James told the kids that he and Karen were going to take a long walk and handed his son the keys to the Lexus so the kids could do whatever they wanted.

They were about an hour into their walk up a trail on a mountain when Karen took a step and the dirt underneath her collapsed. She slid down the mountain about twenty-five feet. James yelled, "Are you okay?" Karen said she was only bruised and was fine. James grabbed his cell phone and called 9-1-1. The woman answered, "Wood County 9-1-1, what is your emergency?" James answered, "My wife slid down a hillside and is trapped on a ledge." The dispatcher asked, "What is your name and where are you located?" James answered, "My name is James Daniels and I have no idea where we are. I am a Cincy cop and you need to ping my phone to determine where we are. We will require an air extraction as the path does not appear to be stable enough to lift her up manually." The dispatcher told James, "Please stay on the line, I will be right back with you sir." When she returned to the line she said, "I just contacted the Urban Search and Rescue team which is two counties from us. The only helicopter near us is the Ohio Highway Patrol and it is in the Dayton, Ohio area searching for a suspect who shot at a trooper. I will attempt to contact the Coast Guard to see if they can offer us assistance. Just be patient, we are working hard to get you help." After a few minutes of silence, the dispatcher told James that the Coast Guard would be sending a chopper, but would not be able to conduct the operation until daybreak because they would not arrive until after darkness. James told her, "I need you to send a unit to my campsite and notify my children of the situation." The dispatcher answered, "Done, just hunker down for the evening and we will call you the moment we can start the rescue."

James removed the backpack he was wearing and withdrew a rescue blanket and emergency snacks that were packed inside. The backpack also had a fifty-foot nylon rope which he wrapped around the blanket and snacks and lowered them down to Karen. He was really surprised at how calm Karen had remained, given all of the stresses of the fall.

James told Karen to wrap the blanket around her completely, covering her head as well. He told her to expel as much air as possible into the blanket as her body temperature breath would warm the inside of the blanket. He tried to find a close alcove to keep the cold air away. As the darkness came, the cold was causing him to shiver uncontrollably. Late into the evening, something flashed in his vision not far from where Karen was sleeping. He shined a flashlight and saw a mountain lion about fifty feet from her. James told Karen to cover her ears and reached into the backpack for his city issued .40 caliber handgun. He fired three shots in the direction of the cat with no intention of hitting it. The loud crack of the shots scared the cat which ran away.

It seemed to be an endless period of time until the first signs of daybreak appeared. His cell phone rang and a male said, “This is the Wood County Sheriff’s Office and we are initiating the rescue now. The chopper should be to your location in minutes.” Just a few minutes later, James could see the Coast Guard copter approaching them and yelled to Karen that help had arrived. She peeked out of her cocoon and smiled and waved.

A rope with a basket dropped down from the helicopter and a male used a rope to rappel to the ground. Karen was loaded onto the basket and it was pulled up to the copter. James watched as Karen was pulled into the inside and let out a sigh of relief. The man who loaded her was pulled up and then dropped down next to James. This time he had an extra belt which he wrapped around James and the two were lifted together. Once in the helicopter, James was wrapped in a warm blanket and he was given an IV with a warmed saline solution to bring up his body temperature. The helicopter landed on the roof at the hospital and he and Karen were taken inside. A deputy sheriff was waiting for them and told them that the kids were being escorted to the hospital by the Sheriff’s Department. They were only there a short time before being released to go home after her abrasions were cleaned and she was given short-term pain killers.

The drive home was noticeably quiet as no one really knew what to say. The kids drove their friends home and James and Karen were tired and just went to bed.

James walked into the District for his shift and made a beeline for the Supervisors Office. When he walked into the office the Sergeant behind the desk looked up and said, "Not interested, go away." James said, "I need a Discharging Firearm form boss." The supervisor stopped what he was doing and asked, "And who did you shoot at Officer?" James smiled meekly and answered, "Not who Sarge, what. I fired three shots at a Mountain Lion that got dangerously close to my wife on Saturday in Wooster, Ohio." The Sergeant said, "This is a prank, right?" "No sir, this was very real" James answered. James went on to tell the Sergeant the whole story and all the sergeant could say was "WOW!" The Sergeant gave James the form and a form to take to the firing range to replace the three bullets he fired. The Sergeant told James to go to the range immediately after roll call. After roll call, James told Frock that they needed to go to the range on orders of the Sergeant. As they made the twenty minute drive, James told Frock the whole story. Frock said, "Did you kill it?" James replied, "Didn't want to kill it, just scare it away and it worked."

The day went by quickly with the two wiring reports and writing two traffic tickets. Frock told James that he would be driving on Tuesday and doing the majority of the work so that he could evaluate James in action. They caught a purse snatching as they walked out of the District. The description of the suspect came out as they were in route and they saw the suspect walking down Twelfth Street. As soon as the suspect saw the cruiser, he started running and Frock jumped out of the car to give chase. James called in the foot pursuit and drove past the suspect to block him off. When the suspect slowed down, Frock tackled him and had him in cuffs before James could get to them. The suspect had a wad of cash and the victim's credit cards in his pocket. They drove back to where the offense occurred and the victim identified the guy as being the man who grabbed her purse. James walked back to the cruiser and told the man he was caught, but the judge might go lighter if the woman got her purse and money back. The suspect agreed to take the two cops back to where he threw the purse and the victim was thrilled to get her property back. When they dropped the prisoner off at the Justice Center, Frock complimented James on the way he was able to get the prisoner to tell them where the purse was. It took almost three hours of the shift to get the prisoner processed and the reports done.

They were patrolling near the river when James saw a man standing on a ledge on the Clay Wade Bailey bridge which connects Cincinnati and Covington, Kentucky. Frock parked the cruiser a safe distance away and the two walked up to where they could talk with the man. James approached slowly and asked, "We are concerned about you sir. Is everything okay?" The man looked at James and said, "I have nothing to live for. My wife left me and I lost my job. Just let me jump." James got a relaxed look on his face and said, "I am a brand new cop and not experienced in this type of situation, but I dealt with a lot of people in my life who had their houses foreclosed and lost everything. Do you have any children?" The man looked down and answered, "Yes, I have a boy and a girl." James said, "Do you think that they love their dad?" The man contemplated for a moment and then said, "Yes, I think so." James leaned back against a pillar and asked, "Wouldn't you like to be there for graduation, their marriages and grandchildren?" The man looked down at the Ohio River below and whispered, "Yes, I think I would like that." The man extended his arm out and James grabbed it and gently brought him back onto the bridge. He was handcuffed and taken to a waiting paramedic unit and was transported to University of Cincinnati Medical Center for a psychiatric evaluation. James rode in the ambulance while Frock followed behind. Frock looked at James as they were leaving the hospital and said, "We need to re-name you Father James, the department priest. That was a helluva job for which you will become a department legend. The rest of the shift went quickly.

When James walked into the District for his shift, he was immediately told to report to the Captain's office. Frock was already seated in the office and James was getting really nervous about what he had done wrong. The Captain told James to go home and put on a suit like he wore when he was in banking and that he and Frock would be on loan to the Central Vice Unit for the day. The Captain told Frock that he would be in uniform and would be in a marked cruiser. The Vice Commander was in his office when the two cops arrived. She told the two cops that there had been a rash of robberies of Johns and that they were occurring all over the city. James would be in an unmarked car and Frock would be in a cruiser because the FTO was always responsible for their recruit. The vice cops were out looking for hookers who matched the description the victims had given. When they found a potential suspect, James would drive to the location and attempt to get solicited. The Captain told James his job was not to arrest the prostitute; it was to locate the robbery team. James was given the keys to a two year old Porsche to use, which had been seized from a drug dealer, for the operation. No sooner than he got into the car, he was sent to just outside downtown to a possible suspect. James slowly drove past the hooker and then went around the block again slowing down. The hooker smiled and James pulled over to the curb. The hooker, wearing a mini-skirt, walked up to the passenger window and bent over to peer inside. She asked him, "So what are you looking for today?" James smiled and answered, "Just looking for some stress relief, I just left a business meeting that was a bitch." The hooker asked, "How do I know you are not a cop?" James reached into his suitcoat and pulled out a business card from his job at Fifth-Third which said, "Vice President Financial Services. The hooker slid into the passenger seat and told James to turn into the alley just down the block and she would take care of his stress needs. Two teams of vice cops set up on both sides of the alley and got out of their vehicles to wait for the next move. Frock was less than half a block away waiting in his marked police car. James stopped in the alley and immediately saw a large African-American male approach the car, the guy pulled a semi-automatic handgun from his belt and told James to give him his wallet. James had been given a wallet containing cash so that he would not lose his real identification should a robbery happen. James held the wallet out the window and calmly said, "Here is the deal. Unless you want to die today, I strongly suggest that you put the gun on the hood of the car. You will be surrounded by cops in the next seconds and they have no sense of humor when a gun is pointed at another cop." The suspect laughed and said, "Man, you ain't no cop." He immediately heard a voice yell, "Drop the gun asshole!" The suspect slowly turned and saw four men with guns pointed at him. He looked back at James and said simply, "Shit, you are a cop!" Two of the vice cops dragged the female from the passenger side of the Porsche, while the other two vice cops and Frock handcuffed the male. James exited the Porsche and there were high-fives all around. James looked at Frock and asked, "What are we supposed to do the rest of the day?" Frock smiled and answered, "Hours of paperwork partner, hours." Frock transported the suspect back to the Vice office and James followed in the Porsche. Frock took the prisoner to jail after he had been interviewed and James was told he was done for the day and to go home. Both cops were told that they receive a commendation for their work.

The rest of the first four weeks of the training went smoothly. As James was preparing to move to his second FTO Frock told him, "You have progressed much better than any of the recruits I have had up to this point. I will not see you again for eight weeks. Call me with who you are assigned to and I will try to give you any helpful tips I have to offer. You need to conform with whatever the FTO wants from you in order to make it through this gauntlet. We can work out any glitches in the last four weeks. You clearly have a future in this agency and you are in a place that you need to be. Just keep your mouth shut and your ears open and in twelve weeks you will have the full status of police officer."

***

James reported for his shift in District working the night shift which was ten until eight. His new FTO was a 24 year old female officer with six years of experience. She was a police cadet when she turned eighteen and graduated the police academy on her twenty first birthday. Brenda Milko was just over five feet tall and weighed just over one hundred pounds. When they got in the cruiser, Milko looked like she could barely see over the steering wheel of the Ford Explorer. She told James that the first week of their time would be foreplay. She just wanted to get to know and understand him before trying to evaluate his ability to be a cop. Their first call was a domestic dispute between a husband and wife. James went to separate the husband, but Milko pushed him out of the way and moved the husband to another room, but in a place where she could keep James in view. James learned that the two had marital problems dating back years. The husband had gone to prison for dealing drugs and had only recently been released. He had been depressed and was drinking, but had not physically abusive to her. She said that it had been a neighbor who called the police, not her. She showed no visible sign of injury and, at this point, no laws had been violated, James heard the husband's voice rising and moved to where he could intervene if necessary. With no crime, the two cops were only there for a short time and left. Milko complimented James on his ability to de-escalate a fluid situation and the fact that he moved toward her when the husband showed aggression.

They made a traffic stop on a car that was weaving. Milko approached the driver while James took a position on the passenger side where he could see the driver's hands. Milko asked the woman driver to get out of the car and she refused. When Milko opened the driver's door, the woman attempted to pull is shut. When Milko turned, she saw James standing next to her and they both pulled the driver from the car and struggled to get her cuffed. The woman tested .16 on a breathalyzer and was charged with Operating a Vehicle While Intoxicated. Processing her took the remainder of the shift. Milko's last words for the night were, "I am going to enjoy working with you. You have a keen sense for situational awareness."

The next night, Milko told James to drive. She showed him all of the main roads that would be needed to get to any call they would receive. They were in the north end of the District when the All County tones dropped advising of a silent holdup alarm at the Carrousel Hotel on Reading Road, just outside the City limits. The two arrived less than one minute later and James parked the cruiser along the side of the building and the two walked around to the front. They looked in a window and saw the suspect pointing a gun at the clerk. James bent down and went under the window to get to the front door while Milko stayed and took a defensive position. When he reached the door, MIlko tapped on the window to distract the suspect who wheeled around pointing the gun toward the window. James hit the suspect like a linebacker hitting a running back, knocking the man to the floor and the gun from his hand. James had the man in cuffs before Milko could get into the lobby. When the Sheriff's car arrived, they turned the prisoner over to him because the offense did not occur within City limits. They were also able to get back on the air to take calls in their beat.

At the end of the first week, the two sat and went over the written evaluation that Milko had written. Her compliments were glowing and there was nothing derogatory in them. James expressed concern that no shortcomings listed might be taken the wrong way by supervisors, but Milko laughed and said, "I have the highest washout rate in the city. If you had screwed up, you would know it. Don't get too comfortable pal, we still have three weeks for you to get on my bad side."

The next night was really quiet until the two left the restaurant where they ate. Communications dispatched them to a pedestrian struck on Reading Road. When they arrived on the scene, they saw a Crown Victoria parked in the southbound lane with flashing emergency blinkers and a Metro bus parked on the northbound side. The victim had been thrown into the grass from the impact. James walked up to the woman driver while Milko went to the woman who had obviously died on impact. The driver told James that she was driving to work when the woman ran into the street apparently to chase the bus. James placed her in the back seat of the cruiser to try to calm her and told her that, because the victim was dead, he needed to inform her of her rights and she might want to speak to a lawyer. The woman waived her right to an attorney and said she was traveling the speed limit when she suddenly saw the victim. She had no opportunity to take evasive action. Milko had called for additional cars to close the four lane highway pending the arrival of the traffic safety unit investigators. Milko found the woman's purse and her driver's license showed the address they were in front of. When the traffic cops arrived, the two cops went into the apartment building and banged on the victim's door. A young female voice on the other side of the door told them that she was not allowed to open the door for anyone, even cops. James found the manager's apartment and woke the manager to get a master key. The two cops entered the apartment and found a twelve year old male and a thirteen year old female hiding in the bedroom. When the two children saw the cops in uniform, they came out from under the bed. The girl told the cops that the woman that was hit was their grandmother and that they lived with her. James asked where their parents were and the boy told him that his mom was in something called WITSEC. James reached for his cell phone and called a number at the FBI that is answered twenty-four hours a day. When the agent answered, James told him, "I am James Daniels, a Cincinnati Police officer and I need am after-hours number for the US Marshall Service. The agent responded, "I am not authorized to give out that number to anyone, but I will call them and they will call you back in the next ten minutes." Ten minutes later the cell phone rang and a female voice said, "This is Deputy Walsh from the Marshal Service, how can I help you?" James explained the situation and told the woman he needed to make contact with the mother.  Walsh said, "Regrettably, that cannot happen. The mother is not in Cincinnati and is part of the Witness Protection Program. Give me an address and we will be there within the hour. About an hour later, two people walked up to the apartment wearing lanyards with a badge saying "U S Marshal Service." They told the two cops that they would take responsibility for the children and reunite them with their mother. On the daily evaluation Milko wrote, "Recruit handled a delicate and complex situation quickly and effectively and was able to bring it to a satisfactory resolution."

The last two weeks ran smoothly and without incident. The two sat in the roll call room at the end of the last shift and Milko said, "I have never said this before, but I learned as much or more from you than anything I was able to teach. You have a skill of de-escalating a stressful situation that I have never seen and I hope you will be teaching that skill at the police academy someday. I wish you the best in the next stage of your training and hope I will get the opportunity to work with you again someday."

***

For phase three James got assigned to the noon to ten shift in District Three. His FTO was a nine year veteran named William Marsh. James called Frock and asked about Marsh. Frock's answer was, "Shit, you could not have drawn a worse cop. Marsh is a mental case who has no business being a cop, much less a trainer. He runs by the seat of his pants and just wants to drink and party with the groupies. Be very careful and make sure your body camera is always on. You need to protect yourself in case he finally does something that will get him fired or worse. They don't call him Wild Bill for nothing!"

When the Sergeant introduced them, Marsh would not even shake hands with James. He just grabbed the Recruit binder from James and walked away. The Sergeant just shrugged his shoulders and told James, "You only have to tolerate him for four weeks. If he gives you a problem, just come to me and I will try to help you resolve it." After roll call, Marsh walked to the cruiser and got in the driver's seat without saying a word. James got into the passenger seat and Marsh drove out of the parking lot to start their shift. Marsh pulled into the drive thru of a White Castle restaurant and ordered a coffee. He did not even ask James if he wanted anything. It was going to be a LONG four weeks.

Just after dark, they received a radio run to Eighth and State Avenue for shots fired at the Detroit Highwaymen motorcycle club clubhouse. Three cruisers arrived almost simultaneously and they could see two men laying on the sidewalk bleeding. James jumped out of the cruiser and checked one man who was obviously dead. Another cop yelled, "This one is dead." Two cops who went around to the rear of the building yelled that they had a dead male in the back. James and two other cops entered the clubhouse with their guns drawn and found a fifth dead man on the floor. There was blood everywhere, but no one else was around. James went to the office where he found the surveillance camera system. He withdrew the cassette from the player and held onto it for the Homicide detectives who he knew would be coming. When a Lieutenant arrived at the scene, James handed over the tape to her. She ordered him to tape off the scene and told other cops to shut down the streets around the clubhouse to protect any possible evidence. He retrieved the yellow crime scene tape from the trunk and wrapped it around a light pole unraveling it as he walked. Out of the corner of his eye he could see the media trucks getting as close as they were allowed and the flood lights of the cameras come on. He was almost to them when a woman with a microphone ran up to him and asked, “What can you tell me about what happened?” James smiled meekly and continued stretching the tape as he walked away. He had not seen his training officer in almost an hour and had no clue where he was. Command staff began showing up in droves including the Police Chief and a couple of Assistant Chiefs. Every time one would pass him, James would salute in recognition of their rank. The Sergeant who conducted the roll call walked up to James and asked, “Where the fuck is your FTO?” James shrugged his shoulders and answered, “No clue, boss.” The sergeant looked at James and said, “When we clear this scene, you are with me. We will resolve this tomorrow and you will be with someone else. I have to determine who on this shift is a trained FTO.” James looked at the Sergeant and said, “Boss, he has my recruit book.”

When James went home and got to bed, he had nightmares about the horrific violence he had witnessed. When he woke up, he made a beeline to see if Dave was at home. The Highway Patrol cruiser was in the driveway, so James knocked on the door. Dave answered and James asked, “Have you got a few minutes?” James asked, “I know that you have seen terrible things over your career and wondered how you are able to handle it?” He went on to explain what transpired at the clubhouse. Dave sat for a moment in silence and then said, “My first fatal crash hit me hard. Two people were killed in a head-on crash on a rural road. I made a decision that whatever happened at work would remain in the police car and I would not bring it home. A dead body is not a human anymore, it is physical evidence. That does not mean that it is not treated with the utmost of respect, but it separates the experience of dealing with a live human. That is how I am able to deal with the horrific things we see. I hope that helps.”

James reported for his shift and was told that he would be assigned to desk duty in the District for his remaining three days and then he would return to his primary FTO for the remainder of his training. He was also told that Marsh had been suspended pending a disciplinary hearing and that he had been removed from the Field Training program.

James answered the telephone calls into the District and served people who walked into the station. Cops came up to him and told him that no one blamed him for what happened to Marsh and that he was lucky to have gotten away from him. James had just completed a telephone call when two men walked up to the window and flashed badges to gain entry into the District. James watched as they went directly to the supervisor’s office. Moments later they came out with a Sergeant who announced, “These two guys are from Internal Investigation Section and they want to talk to you. I will cover the desk until you get back.”

The three men walked to a conference room and one of the cops pointed to a chair for James to sit down. He said,

"My name is Sergeant Walter and this is Sergeant Lee. We are from the Internal Investigation Section and have been sent here by the Police Chief to get a statement about last night. You are not in any trouble. Tell us about meeting Officer Marsh and what transpired the rest of the evening." Sergeant Walter pulled out a pocket tape recorder and set it on the table.

James said, "The Sergeant introduced us and Officer Marsh took my recruit binder. (He left out the part where Marsh would not shake his hand and the stop at the restaurant) We got into the car and there were no words exchanged. When we arrived at the homicide, I went to check on one of the victims and lost track of him. I never saw him after that."

The headhunters thanked James and left. James returned to the desk.

***

James reported back to District One where Frock was waiting for him. He told James, "Word flew all over the city about you and Marsh. No one is holding you responsible for any of it. Let's get back to work and get through the rest of your training, so you become just another one of us."

After roll call, the two walked out to their cruiser and started their patrol. Frock asked, "You ready for coffee partner?" They went to a drive thru and Frock said he wanted a blow-by-blow of the events of the evening. James laughed and told Frock about Marsh getting coffee and not asking if James wanted anything.

They were dispatched to control traffic at the scene of a two alarm fire in an apartment building at Twelfth and Vine Street. When they arrived, flames were shooting out of the roof of the structure and people were yelling that there were people trapped inside. Frock and James ran into the building which was filling with smoke and began banging on apartment doors. They knocked on a door and heard the sound of a woman moaning, so Frock kicked the door open. The two saw a woman in her seventies laying on the floor coughing and gagging. They picked her up and Frock carried her out the front door to a waiting paramedic unit. As soon as she was on a gurney, they returned, but the smoke was too dense and they could not enter. Firemen with breathing masks entered the hallway and did a room by room search for victims. On the second floor the firemen found an elderly man who had perished from smoke inhalation. As soon as the two cops heard about it Frock said, "We did everything we could, it is not your fault." The words sounded hollow to James, who felt that it was their job to save the man. They stayed and directed traffic away from the fire for the next three hours. They were relieved and stopped at a restaurant to eat. Frock told James, "You cannot take this personally. You cannot save everyone in this life and we did actually save a woman's life today, it is a good day." They wrote one traffic citation and the day was over. On the drive home, James thought about what his neighbor had told him and left the incident in the car.

When James arrived for his shift, Frock told him that he put in the paperwork for the completion of the Field Training and that it was up to the FTO Coordinator to sign off. Frock said, "If the paperwork is approved, you will be assigned to a different District and will be on your own. We should know by the end of the week.

James was walking on Cloud Nine the whole shift which was mundane. Frock told James, "I really hope that someday we will get to work together again. It has been a truly great experience for me." Two days later, the notification was signed off on and James was assigned to the afternoon shift in District Five starting the following week. His new off days would be Tuesday, Wednesday and Thursday.

## CHAPTER FOUR

James reported to work and sat down in the roll call room waiting for his assignment. The Sergeant introduced him to the room full of cops and told him he would be working 5208 with Officer Dahlia Jones. Jones raised her hand and smiled so James would know who she was. Jones was just under six feet tall and had played college basketball for Duke University and then two seasons as a professional in the WNBA before she was cut from the team in Dallas. She returned home and joined the Cincinnati Police Department just over seven years ago.

When they got to the cruiser, Jones asked, "Do you want to drive?" James shook his head no saying, "I don't know any of the streets so I will learn better from the passenger side." Jones said, "This beat covers the northwestern part of the District to the city limits. It is bounded by Green Township, Colerain Township and Springfield Township. Springfield and Colerain have their own police departments, while Green shares policing with the Sheriff's Patrol. She showed James the main thoroughfares which are Colerain Avenue that runs north and south and North Bend Road that runs east and west. She told him he could get anywhere he needed to go using those streets. They wrote one ticket for a stop sign and investigated one traffic crash in the first two hours of the shift. Jones told James, "The bosses expect one ticket per shift. Some call that a quota, but in reality, if you do not witness a single traffic violation in a ten hour shift, you had your head up a cow's ass getting a milkshake." That made James bust out in laughter.

The two were driving up a residential street when the All County tones sounded. The broadcast said that Covington, Kentucky police were in pursuit of a black pick-up truck northbound on I-75 entering Ohio and that it was wanted for an armed robbery. The two listened as the second set of tones said the vehicle was entering I-74 and was getting off at Colerain Avenue. Jones headed toward North Bend and Colerain to set up a roadblock. When she arrived, there were already two Green Township cruisers at the intersection. The three cruisers blocked the northbound lanes of the four lane highway waiting for the pursuit to get to them. When the truck approached with a line of police cars behind it, the driver swerved into the southbound lanes almost hitting a car head-on. Jones let out a yell and said, "Its rock and roll time, let's party." She and the two Green Township cars joined in the chase that went up Colerain Avenue through Green Township and into Colerain Township. Colerain Township Police, North College Hill Police and the Hamilton County Sheriff's Patrol now joined in and there were fourteen police cars behind the truck. The driver pulled into a small shopping center and the two occupants bailed out, each running in a different direction. Jones and James followed one in their cruiser and saw a Springfield Township canine unit arrive on the scene. The cruiser was still moving as the Township cop hit the release on the back door and the dog came out at a dead run. Jones and James jumped out and gave chase and heard a loud scream from behind the building. When they rounded the corner, they could see the suspect fighting the dog and losing badly. James started to run toward the suspect, but Dahlia grabbed his arm and said, "That dog don't know or care that you are a cop. You get near him and you get bit." It was just a few seconds later that the dog's handler came around the corner. He tried to call the dog off the suspect, but the dog was having none of it. The fight was still on and the dog was winning. The handler ran up and grabbed the dog's collar and pulled it off the suspect who was bleeding profusely from the multiple bites. James smiled as Dahlia handcuffed the suspect announcing, "Good Banacek. GOOD dog." A call came out for a rescue unit for the other suspect whose head apparently ran into a metal flashlight multiple times. The canine handler requested a second paramedic unit for the suspect bitten by the canine. Both suspects were now in custody and the two cops could return to the city. Dahlia looked at James and asked, "How the hell did you know the dog's name?" James smiled and said, "I got to see him in action once before when I was doing my ride along in the police academy. He ate that guy alive too!"

As they drove around, Dahlia explained that new cops always got second shift because it screwed up the day for most. She liked it because it let her take her son to school and her husband would pick him up. The shift assignments were for one year and went by seniority. The same applied to beat assignments. New cops would be skippers, which means they cover a beat on the off days of an officer. It usually takes two to three years of seniority to get a permanent beat, unless it is a beat no one wants. There are a few shit beats in the District, but they will not be up until October. That is also the time you can change

Districts if you want, or the bosses can banish you to some far-away place if they don't like you.

As the day came to a close, Dahlia said, "We had a pretty good first day together partner, I am off the next three, so you will probably be assigned to someone else. I am looking forward to what the next time brings."

James was teamed with a twenty-three year veteran to beat 5202. This covered the western side of the University of Cincinnati campus. Dave Dingle laughed when they got in the cruiser telling James that he was only two years older than James. When they arrived at the campus, Dingle said, "I have been running this beat for the last three years and it is mostly dealing with the brats who attend college here and think their shit don't stink. The former police chief of the University created a program where a campus cop would be partnered with one of us. If we could not lock the little monkeys up, the campus cop would hand them an administrative violation and that worked really well. When that chief retired, the entire agency went to hell in a handbasket.

Dingle drove James down the long hill of Ravine Street and told James about a cop who ran the beat for twenty years. Frank (Pappy) Feldhaus retired at sixty-eight years old and knew every person on the street by their name. He was a legend in the Cincinnati Police Department.

Dingle drove James to where a University of Cincinnati police officer shot and killed a man on a traffic stop. The campus cop was charged with Murder and tried twice.

Both cases resulted in a mistrial because both juries could not reach a unanimous verdict.

James liked the fact that Dingle was low key and calm about being a cop and knew how to deal with people. This was the kind of cop that James hoped to be.

It was coming up on eleven in the evening when the radio cracked out, "Attention all cars, all departments, an all-county broadcast. Off duty officer needs assistance skating rink at 912 East McMillan in District Four." Dingle looked at James and said, "We are about three miles away, but there will be District Four cars there within a minute or so. Two minutes later the call was repeated with the addition, "Officer still needs assistance 921 East McMIllan." Dingle jumped on the radio saying. "5202 show us in route." James activated the overhead lights and siren as communications broadcast, "Cars on the scene still requesting assistance special attention District One and Five cars. Any available units respond. When the two got to the 900 block, they saw two lines of marked police cars parked in the street. They had to park over a block away and they ran toward the skating rink. Officers were coming out of the rink with prisoners in handcuffs. The two entered the rink and immediately were attacked by two males. Dingle punched one and James tackled the other. The radio was still requesting additional units respond to the rink as cops were screaming into the radio, "Officers need assistance, send help!" Dingle and James got their suspects in cuffs and had to drag them out of the rink. They would later find out that the disc jockey made an announcement that the rink was closing and the crowd of several hundred yelled, "Shut the fuck up and keep on playing." The rink had paid for one uniformed off-duty cop to provide security for the event and he was overwhelmed quickly. The off-duty cop was transported to the hospital for injuries suffered from the attack.

James went home from each shift reminding himself how lucky he was in being coupled with good cops who cared. He didn't like to talk about work at home remembering to leave the job in the car and just focus on family. He missed having dinner with them because of the shift work, but always talked to the family about their experiences, needs and desires. The one thing that the job brought was a marked increase in his sex life. Whether it came from being in better physical condition or was a result of being a cop, he and his wife came to enjoy intimate contact more often and it was more pleasurable. Prior to joining the police department, sex was sporadic and not much fun.

James reported for his shift and was given a solo car for the first time. His beat was the College Hill section of the District and he was a bit nervous about not having someone to answer his questions and help him navigate through calls. He had only been out about an hour when he was dispatched to a domestic violence run to back up Dahlia on Bahama Terrace, an apartment complex in Mount Airy. Dahlia arrived first and James got there a couple of minutes later. The two walked up to the front door of the apartment to speak to the female who called 9-1-1. They entered the apartment and the male half immediately became combative. James put out a call for assistance as the struggle went out the rear door onto the grass. James was punched in the face and Dahlia was grabbed and her head smashed against the brick wall. The female half joined the fight and the male grabbed Dahlia's Taser. James could hear the sirens of responding units, but it felt like everything was running in slow motion. James was bleeding from the face as the first two cops arrived to help. It took several minutes to get both into custody. Dahlia was transported to the hospital to be treated for a head injury and James was treated by paramedics at the scene. Both suspects were charged with assault on a police officer, a felony in Ohio and the male was charged with robbery for taking Dahlia's Taser. James worked the balance of his shift with a headache.

James was able to get into a routine of running different beats each night and the young cops were adjusting to him. They asked him several times to go to a cop bar for drinks after the shift, but he always politely declined, telling them he was too old for that kind of life. He learned to watch his Mobile Digital Computer to see what the officers around him were dealing with and always would arrive to back other officers up before they called for help. That caused the other cops to respect him even though he was not a party animal like they were.

***

In late August the posting for the system wide changes appeared on the bulletin board. James put in a transfer request to the Business District on nights. The request was granted and he was assigned to downtown beginning the first Sunday in October. He was immediately sent to training on the operation of the Segway, a two wheel motorized scooter which he would ride around the entertainment district at the river. There would be large crowds after Cincinnati Reds baseball games at Great American Ballpark or Cincinnati Bengal football games at Paul Brown Stadium. He liked the fact that he could ride the Segway into the parking garages for the Stadiums and was able to catch several car break-ins in progress. His arrest statistics caught the attention of the Business District Commander, who made it a point to single him out to the rest of the shift at roll call. As the Commander was speaking, James was visibly blushing and was razzed by the other cops, who said he was making them look bad.

James would leave roll call and grab the Segway to write parking tickets in the entertainment district. He was not happy that parking at an expired meter cost the owner of the vehicle forty-five dollars, but the city wanted the enforcement, so James did his job. He would then ride the Segway into the indoor parking garages looking to catch car burglars. He rode into the parking garage at Third and Broadway and went up to the third level where he a couple smoking a joint. When the male saw him, he dropped the joint to the floor. James wrote both a ticket for possession of marijuana and handed the male the ticket book for him to sign the citation. The male refused to sign the ticket so James explained, "You are not admitting guilt, you are only agreeing that you received a copy of the citation. Refusing to sign will result in a physical arrest." The male suspect demanded that a supervisor be called. Police policy states, "When a citizen requests a police supervisor be called, officers shall immediately contact police communication and a supervisor shall be dispatched." It took about ten minutes for the supervisor to arrive. The suspect told the Sergeant, "The United States Supreme Court has ruled that a police officer must be legally where they are to witness a crime. This is a private garage." The Sergeant smiled and replied, "The Cincinnati Police Department has a letter on file from the Western and Southern Life Insurance Company designating every Cincinnati police officer as an agent of the owner. Therefore, the officer was lawfully where he was. You have two options, sir: you can come to the District and I will show you the letter or you can plead not guilty in Court and we will bring the letter. As an agent of the owner, I am ordering you to leave the premises or you will be arrested for criminal trespassing." When the couple had left the garage, the Sergeant said, "You lucked out. You do not have the authority to enter private property without an invitation. Stick to the public parking garages and continue doing a GREAT job!" With that, the Sergeant and went back to his cruiser.

***

Every Christmas season, the Cincinnati Police form a task force of plainclothes officers to patrol the streets looking for criminal activity. James was assigned to the team with a partner to patrol the downtown area in an unmarked car. The two were driving down Sixth Street when James saw a man coming out of a Chinese restaurant with a gun in one hand and a brown bag in the other. The man ran to a running car parked in the front of the restaurant. The car took off and the two cops gave chase, activating the blue lights in the grill and the siren. James was the passenger and called the chase as it headed toward Interstate 75. Multiple cars blocked the intersection at Ninth and Central Avenue. The officers yelled out for the occupants of the car to exit the vehicle and heard two gunshots. A SWAT team was called while everyone held their positions. There was no movement inside the car and James slowly moved toward the rear of the suspect car. When he could see inside, he saw a dead male in the front seat in an apparent suicide as no shots were fired by the police. The cops had to wait for the Homicide detectives to arrive. The detectives seemed leery that the suspect was not killed by a police bullet. All of the cops at the scene were swabbed for gunshot residue to rule out that any of them fired the shot. The autopsy showed that the suspect did, in fact, shoot himself. At the end of the shift, James was still scratching his head as to what would make someone kill himself.

After three weeks of the holiday season, James returned to uniform and his Segway.

## CHAPTER FIVE

James enjoyed the experiences that the business district offered, but wanted more interaction with the people who actually live in the city. He put in for a transfer to District Two which would be a closer drive from home that he could get to from Interstate 71 and was more residential based. His request was granted and he started the first Sunday in October.

James was teamed with Charley Spellman, a twenty-one year veteran working the farthest point in the city, an area called Mount Washington. When they got into the cruiser, Spellman said, "You are not exactly a kid who needs to learn, so why did they team you with me? What, if anything, do you want me to teach you?" James smiled and answered, "I want to learn how to get from point A to point B but, more importantly, I want to understand the lay of the land. I transferred out of the Business District to get to patrol residential areas and actually interact with the people who live in the city." Spellman thought for a moment and said, "I am not sure why you care, but I will try my best to acquaint you with the intricacies of my beat. The two drove across the Beechmont Levy, the connector between the east side of the City and the County line. Spellman told James that the levy was a race course for speeders and it was like fishing in a barrel full of fish to catch them. When they reached Corbly Avenue, Spellman showed James the apartment buildings full of lower income residents who drank and fought on a regular basis, He told James, "The closest city car for backup is six to eight miles away. We get our help from the Sheriff's

Department, who have four cars on the street within a three mile radius. Spellman drove James down to the river where there was a horse race track and an amusement park. There was also a night club which could draw as many as one thousand people on a given night. Spellman was talkative the whole night and told James that District Two had the least number of calls for service in the city and that it was known as the retirement center for lazy cops. Spellman said, "The bosses here are really low key and that is a good thing. Don't make waves and you will fare well here."

James was assigned to a single person can running beat eight serving the Oakley neighborhood. He was driving east on Madison Road when he got a call of a domestic violence. When he arrived at the apartment building, he was told that the problem was on the top floor. James walked up the steps to the third floor and was met by a Hispanic woman. She told James that her boyfriend had left two days earlier and then returned today demanding money. When she told him that she had none to give, he grabbed her six year old son and told her to go out and find some money. James asked the woman the name of the man and the name of her son. He also asked where they were in the apartment. The woman told him that the boyfriend's name was Paulie and the son was Pedro. She said they were seated on a couch in the back half of the apartment. James punched the transmit button on his radio and said, "Car 5208, start me some cars to 1345 Henderson Avenue, I have a possible hostage situation." James slowly opened the door of the apartment to locate the suspect and saw that he was far enough away making it safe to enter. He saw the adult holding a knife to the child's neck. He told Paulie, "You need to put down the knife and release the child. There are more cops coming and this will not end well for you if you don't." Paulie got up off the couch with the child and backed away from James. James said, "There is a SWAT team coming and they will have a sniper who will put a bullet into your head if you are near the window. This is not worth dying for." Paulie immediately moved away from the window to a corner of the room. James spoke softly when he said, "Paulie, if you can see out of the window, a sniper will be able to see you. I do not want to have to call for the coroner who will bring a stinky black bag to put your body into. At the instant that you die, you will piss and shit in your pants and they will put you on a table naked and wash you down before they put you in a vault overnight. Is today the day you want to die?" Paulie could hear the sounds of sirens approaching and heard cops yelling "Everything okay in there?" James told the cops to stay in the hallway and he would yell if he needed them. Paulie looked confused and said, "Give me your gun or I will kill the boy." James softly said, "Not going to happen pal, there is a SWAT sniper getting ready to take your head off. The clock is ticking." Paulie dropped the knife and released the child and James called for the cops in the hallway. He was taken into custody without incident.

It took James almost three months to feel like he understood the layout of the numerous neighborhoods in District Two. There was the old money section called Hyde Park, the blue collar special area of Oakley. Each area having its own personality and needs.

## CHAPTER SIX

James arrived at the District for his shift and went directly to the Captain's office. He presented the Captain with a binder containing a fifteen page proposal to create a position titled Community Service Officer. The proposal detailed the tasks that the CSO would perform which would include: Being the District representative at the sixteen neighborhood council meetings and report to the Captain their concerns; handle quality of life calls that the street cops call garbage runs; and form a partnership with Maslow's Army (a homeless advocacy group), United Way, The Free Store and Crossroads Church to address the concerns of the homeless in the District. The Captain took the binder and promised to read it within the next couple of days. Five days passed and James was feeling that the proposal was being ignored. He received a call from communications telling him to return to the District. When he arrived, the Sergeant told him to report to the Captain's office. He walked into the office and the Captain pointed to a chair for him to sit down. She said, "I completely read your proposal three times in order to fully understand it before taking any action. I am forwarding it to the Assistant Chief who oversees the operations of this department with a letter of endorsement attached. I cannot give you a timeline on any action from the Ivory Tower, but I am sure it will reach the Chief. James wanted to jump out of the chair and hug the Captain, but common sense got in the way and he just left saying, "Thank you."

***

James reported for his shift and was told to report to the Captain's office. When he walked into the office, the Captain had an ear-to-ear smile on her face. She handed James a memo from the Police Chief stating that his proposal had been approved for a six month pilot beginning the first of the next month. The Captain told him that they would need to find him an office, get him a separate phone line and find a desk. They walked around the District until they found a suitable space and then returned to her office. She told James, "There are few issues that we need to resolve. I will let you flex your hours so you can meet the needs of the position, but you cannot exceed forty hours without approval and the collective bargaining agreement with the FOP will not allow you to work without getting paid. You will have a marked car solely for your use so that you can equip it with whatever you need. Sadly, I cannot authorize it as a take-home vehicle. You will continue to run a beat until the first of the month and I want you to remember that you are a Police Officer first and a social worker second. I expect you to cover other officers should the situation arise. Do we understand each other?" James smiled and answered, "Clear as a bell Captain."

James would bring things from home to fill the office when he reported for his shift. He brought a white board that he could write his itinerary on and pictures of his family to put on his desk. The Captain ordered him business cards with his name and position of 'COMMUNITY SERVICE OFFICER."

On his first day in the new position, James called each of the social service agencies to come to the District for a strategy meeting. All of the agencies agreed to attend. He walked out to his cruiser and turned on the Mobile Digital Computer to see six quality of life calls that he needed to address. The first call was to a residence which had failed to cut their grass. He contacted police communications section to give the car assigned the run a disregard and that he would handle it. When he arrived, it was clear that the house was abandoned and that he would need to locate the owner to resolve the problem. The County Auditor records showed that the property was in foreclosure and was in the control of the Fifth-Third Bank. When he returned to the District, James called the vice president of the property section of the bank and told him that the problem needed to be resolved. He gave the bank one week to get the problem resolved.

His next call was to a house with trash all over the property. The woman who answered the front door told James that she was a renter and it was not her responsibility to keep the property clean. James told her that she had one week to clean the property or she could tell a judge that it was not her responsibility. She cussed him out and slammed the door in his face. When he checked back two days later, all of the debris had been removed.

His next call was to a property with junk cars parked in the grass. The owner of the property told James that he was repairing the vehicles, so they were not junk. James smiled and calmly said, “So you have a business license and this property is zoned for business, sir?" The man grimaced and replied, "I was not aware that I need a business license." James gave the man one week to remove the cars or he would tow all of the vehicles and let the man get them back from a Court.

James returned to the District to write a daily activity report which would be given to the Captain at the end of each week.

On the second day, James handled the other three quality of life calls and then drove down to a homeless encampment in an underpass under Interstate 71. He counted eighty people living in tents and tarps. He wanted to simply introduce himself to as many of the residents as possible and tell them he cared about their plight. He got the response he expected, in that they were not at all receptive to any cops. This was probably because their experiences with law enforcement were almost always negative. James told whoever would listen, "I am not here to bust anyone, but I will say up front that I will arrest anyone who has open warrants or commits a crime. Other than that, I am not interested in your drug use or alcohol and I am not going to force you out of this life if that is what you choose, but I will make options available in the coming weeks."

On the way back to the District to complete the day's paperwork, a radio call for a silent alarm at the PNC Bank on Madison Road came out. Being only a mile from that, James hit the lights and headed to the bank. He arrived just as four men came out the front door wearing black masks over their faces. The four saw the police car and started shooting, actually hitting the cruiser with four shots. They jumped into a waiting car in front of the bank and drove away. James jumped on the radio saying, "2002 emergency, I have been fired on by the robbery suspects. I am in pursuit of five suspects operating a black jeep northbound on Edwards Road toward Interstate 71. At least four of the suspects are armed with handguns and have fired shots at police." The tones dropped and the dispatcher said, Attention all cars, all departments, Cincinnati police in pursuit of aggravated robbery suspects northbound on Edwards toward I-71." The suspects got onto northbound Interstate 71 and police cars from multiple jurisdictions joined James. The Ohio Highway Patrol got into the chase and performed the Parallel Intervention Technique called the PIT maneuver. The trooper used the right side of his cruiser to push the left side of the Jeep causing it to rotate and spin out. The cops jumped out of their cruisers with tactical rifles and the suspects surrendered without further shots being fired. After everything calmed down a trooper walked up to James and patted him on the back. It was his neighbor who had never actually seen James in his police uniform.

James could not drive back to the District because his car was smoking from two bullets striking the radiator. The left headlight was blown out and a bullet entered the right side of the windshield. James was not really scared until he saw how close the rounds actually got. He shivered and shook on the drive home.

## CHAPTER SEVEN

James set up the conference room for the twelve anticipated participants in the initial meeting of the homeless advocate meeting, and was surprised when eighteen showed up. He had to scramble to find six available chairs.

James had done a Power Point presentation to facilitate the issues that he believed they would be facing and brought a legal pad to record the new issues they would think of. He opened the meeting by saying the goal of this group would be to address the multi-faceted issues that these people face on a daily basis without alienating them and causing them to run. The question was how to give them the best life they can have within whatever their limitations are.

He put up a slide in the presentation listing some of the issues to be addressed. They were: Blankets and winter clothing, food, a safe and clean area for them to live, healthcare, and mental illness treatment. He then came up with his suggestions to fill those needs. He suggested that Crossroads Church send volunteers to clean up the underpass these people call home. He would then have the City Sanitation Department pick up the collected trash. Maslow's Army would work with the individual residents to identify issues they may have. United Way would provide the mental health professionals to provide service to any who want it. James would get one of the hospitals to bring their mobile healthcare recreational vehicles to provide health services. The Food bank would provide items such as peanut butter, jelly and crackers for the residents to serve as a stop-gap for the days when they have no food. Someone would need to step up to provide blankets and winter coats for the winter, which can be grueling in Cincinnati.

When he was done, he opened the meeting up to all of the groups and the discussion got very lively with brainstorming ideas. When it came time for lunch, James ordered pizza for all of the attendees, which he paid for out of his own pocket. James pushed hard that he did not want to force these people into something they did not want and that the Police Department would still enforce violations of law such as theft and assault. That portion was non-negotiable.

A second meeting was set up for the following month to give time for everyone to decide what involvement they chose to have. When the meeting was over, James created a complete report for the Captain which would then be forwarded to the Chief.

Having held many meetings while he worked for the bank, he knew that the first step had been taken, but there would be many setbacks to come. He called his wife and asked her to speak to the people at P&G to get personal care items like toothpaste and toothbrushes, soap, deodorant, and feminine hygiene products donated for this project.

James drove down to the encampment to check on the welfare of the people. When he arrived, he was told that a resident had not come out of his tent in three days. James got to the tent and the smell of a decaying body was prominent. He entered the tent and it was readily apparent that the man who appeared to be in his fifties was dead. James called the Communication Section and had them notify the coroner to send the van out to remove the corpse. An hour later the Sheriff's truck arrived and the inmates removed the male to be taken back to the coroner for an autopsy. No one knew his name or if he had any family to notify. James felt sad that none of the other residents seemed at all concerned that one of their own died.

James left the encampment and was returning to the District when a call came out of an active shooter at Withrow High School on Madison Road. When he was riding with Officer Spellman he was told the history of the school. Built in the 1950s, it housed over one thousand students from some of the city's toughest neighborhoods. Spellman told a story about responding to a burglar alarm at the school with four other cruisers. One of the cops saw the burglar running down a hall so a canine was requested. Four canine units ended up searching the school, but the burglar somehow got away. They learned that the school has five sub-levels and apparently the burglar knew how to access them because he was later seen on video running across a field. James pulled up and entered a side door of the school. As soon as he reached the hallway, he heard gunshots but, due to the echo, had no idea where they were coming from. Communications broadcast that a teacher was down outside the science room, so James called and asked for directions to that area. The radio was dead silent. James moved slowly down the hallway and found two students hunkered down in an alcove. He quietly asked them where the science room was located and they told him to go to the end of the hall, turn right to the end of the hall and turn left. James was still hearing sporadic gunshots and had to move slowly. He came to a hall and saw the male teacher laying on the floor outside of a room. He moved toward the downed person when he saw a male in a gray hoodie come out of an alcove and run down a hall. The male turned and fired two shots at James with a semi-automatic handgun. James also fired two shots, but the suspect turned the corner. James jumped on the radio with," 2002 emergency traffic. Shots fired in the hallway outside the science room. Suspect is a male, approximately five feet ten inches wearing a gray hoodie and blue jeans. I fired shots but do not believe I hit the suspect and there is a male down at my location bleeding in the chest area from a single gunshot. I am going after the suspect. When James reached the end of the hallway, he laid flat to peek around the corner because the suspect, if in the hallway, would be ready to shoot at chest level. When James peeked down the hall, the suspect saw him and immediately fired more shots. James moved to the other side of the hallway and stepped out firing two shots down the hallway, both of which took effect. One hit the chest while the other entered the suspect's forehead. James slowly approached the downed male and kicked the handgun away and rolled the suspect over to place handcuffs on him. Then he checked for a pulse and found none. He got on the radio telling Communications saying, "2002, suspect is down in front of Room 129. Unknown if there are other suspects. I am returning to the downed man at the science room and need paramedics to meet me. Four men came running down the hallway, Two cops and two paramedics. They were followed by a six person tactical team and a canine. James took the SWAT cops down to where the suspect was neutralized and told them that there had been no shots since the suspect was downed. The SWAT commander told James to return to his cruiser and await the arrival of the Homicide Unit. When James walked out of the school, there were at least twenty police cars and police brass everywhere. There were media trucks parked in the grass areas all around the school. A Lieutenant walked over and asked James what had happened. When he saw that James was nervous, he smiled and said, "I understand your concerns since it is your career and freedom at stake. But it is not an issue in this shooting because this individual was clearly an imminent threat which had to be dealt with immediately. I need enough information for the Chief to brief the media monkeys and no, we will not be giving out your name." James gave the Lieutenant a condensed explanation and was told to wait for the Homicide dicks to arrive. Ten minutes later a man and a woman in business suits walked up and introduced themselves to James. The male, named Rudy Grenke, told James, "You have a right to have an attorney present before we ask you any questions and, if you choose, have up to seventy-two hours to answer our questions per the collective bargaining agreement. We also need your firearm for evidence purposes." James was confused by what he was told and decided to ask to talk to a FOP Attorney. He reached for his gun and was told they did not need it until they got to the Criminal Investigation Section and that James would be issued a different weapon before we return you to the District. Someone else will take your cruiser back to the District."

When they arrived at CIS, James was given a number to call for the FOP. He was told to say nothing until the attorney arrived. The homicide cops got him coffee and talked to him about his homeless project while they awaited the arrival of counsel. The attorney came into the room and the two detectives left. James walked the attorney through his actions step-by-step. The attorney left the room and came back with the two detectives. He told the detectives that James would provide the detectives a written statement within the next three days and that the interview was now over. The faces of the homicide cops showed that they were okay with that. When they walked out of the interview room a Sergeant walked over and handed James a replacement handgun and a full magazine to load it. The sergeant had James sign for the weapon and told him that he would transport James back to the District and that he would be placed on Administrative Leave pending his visit to the police psychologist. On the drive back James asked, "Do we know anything about the suspect Sarge?" The Sergeant told James that the suspect was a nineteen year old former student who had been expelled from the school one month earlier and that the suspect had killed one teacher and wounded seven other students. The investigation was not nearly over but it appeared that the suspect was acting alone. When they arrived at the District James was told that he would receive a call for an appointment with the psychologist and that he would receive full pay for the time he was off.

When James arrived home, Karen was watching the television news about the shooting. She could see in his face that there was something wrong and asked, "Were you there?" James nodded yes and she said, "There is something you are not telling me. What the hell happened?" James said, "I had to shoot a nineteen year old kid. I am on paid Administrative Leave until I see the police psychologist." Karen hugged him as he shivered and cried. It was the first time that he could let loose of his feelings. The two were in the house alone as both of the kids were in dorms in college out of state. They ate dinner in front of the television as the local news focused on the school shooting and the interview with the Police Chief. James had difficulty sleeping and Karen called off work to be with him at all times.

The next morning James received a call from the FOP lawyer to come to his office to write the statement for the Homicide Unit. Karen went along and sat with him as James spoke into a recorder which would then be transcribed by a secretary. James was told to take Karen our for breakfast and return to sign the statement.

The two got home just in time for the noon local news. They saw the Police Chief's press conference where the Chief lauded the courage of the officer who they were still declining to identify. After the news Karen said, "He just validated that everything you did was right."

James called the office of the police psychologist and was scheduled for an appointment the next morning. Karen told James, "I am going with you, even if I cannot sit in on the meeting."

Dr. Don greeted the two when they arrived at his office. He smiled and said, "Karen, I need a few minutes with James alone and then you can sit in on any further conversation. I will have a secretary bring you back as soon as I can. The two men walked back into the secure area and Dr. Don said with a big smile, "I gave up on couches, no one would lay down on them. Pick any chair you want. What I want to know is what you are feeling right now." James answered, "To be honest, I do not know what I am feeling. The suspect gave me no choice but to shoot. I do not feel badly about having to take his life, but feel that he made the decision that forced me to do what I did." Dr. Don stuck his head out the door and told the secretary to bring Karen back. When they were both in the room, Dr. Don said, "What, if I can ask Karen, are you feeling at the moment?" She had tears in her eyes and answered, "I am only concerned about James, the rest is someone else's problem." The interview lasted just over one hour and Dr. Don told the couple, "It will take two to three days for my report to make it through the system, but I will be recommending that you be returned to duty. If you experience any issues dealing with all of this, call my office twenty-four hours a day and I will get back to you. I am here to help you. I am not the enemy. Everything that is said here, stays here."

# CHAPTER EIGHT

When James walked into the District, the cops started clapping and walked over to shake his hand. A few asked for details of what had happened, but James would just smile and say, "Not something I want to talk about." James was still having nightmares of seeing the dead eyes of the young man staring up at him.

He arrived at his office and saw stacks of boxes against the wall. The phone showed twenty-seven messages and his email showed forty new messages. James stopped for a moment to do what he had done many times in his business life. He needed to prioritize the tasks. He started by listening to all of the voice mail messages which were from members of his recruit class, police academy instructors, and FTOs, all of which were wishing him well. Next, he went to the boxes which were marked, "P", "J" and "C" to indicate peanut butter, jelly and crackers. Last, he opened all of the emails which, again, were mostly well-wishers. There were a few from the organizations working with him on his homeless project telling him what actions they had taken while he was off work. Crossroads Church had cleaned the area and left the packaged trash to be picked up. They also placed trash receptacles with plastic liners for the residents to use. United Way sent several mental health professionals to the site and they met with each of the people who lived there. Some declined any assistance while others accepted limited help. James was disappointed that no one had been able to address the blanket and winter coat issue, although one suggested that he make contact with St. Vincent DePaul charity.

James broke open the boxes and separated the items for dispersal, He put a number on the bottom of each of the sets so that, if stolen, the owner could be identified. When he completed that, he found two uniform cops in the District and got them to help him load the boxes into his cruiser. He also loaded the personal care items that Karen had gotten P&G to donate into the cruiser and then drove to the homeless camp. When he arrived, he saw full bags of trash so he called the City Sanitation Department to send a small truck to pick them up.

The people in the camp were happy to receive the food and toiletries. He took the opportunity to spend a few minutes with each and told them he was working on getting them winter clothing and blankets. The number of people in the camp had dropped by a few who decided to accept help or had just moved on.

James left the camp and drove to Seven Hills High School, a private school located less than one mile from the camp. He got the school to agree to allow the people from the camp to shower in the locker rooms on a Saturday as long as the Cincinnati Police would provide security. James contacted the city bus company to provide an Access van to transport the people to and from the school. James would have to change his off days so that overtime would not come into play. He would also have to have the Captain sign-off on detailing a female officer for the women's locker room.

While he was immersed in his project, he still had the fourteen neighborhood council meetings to attend and address their concerns. James attended the Evanston council meeting and listened to a woman rail about speeding on her residential street. Two days later James signed out a radar unit and went to the street during the hours she identified. James smiled when the first speeder he stopped was the woman who complained. She told him, "You were supposed to catch the people who don't live on the street. James answered, "Go to Court and tell the judge that the speed limit does not apply to you and maybe it will be dismissed." James wrote nine tickets for speeding in the three hours he was there. He got an email from the Captain saying simply, "Job well done officer."

James contacted the University of Cincinnati Medical Center to arrange for them to bring their mobile medical recreational vehicle to the camp. They agreed as long as he would be present for the entire time. The medical team found the expected issues: head lice, diabetes, and all but one female tested positive for a sexually transmitted disease. The only problem came when a male tested positive for a highly communicable strain of hepatitis. When the medical people told him that he needed to be placed into an isolation unit at the hospital, the fight was on. He struck one nurse and James had to Tase him. A rescue unit was called and the man had to be physically restrained onto the gurney. This caused consternation among the other people in the camp. James had to explain to each person that the man presented a danger to all of them. The man died in the isolation unit two days later.

***

The six month trial of the pilot program was coming quickly and James went to work on the final report. He wanted it to be comprehensive and fair, highlighting the good points and not hiding the shortcomings. The final report was just over two hundred pages and detailed all of the actions of each of the agencies that participated. As far as the Police Department was concerned, the value was overwhelming. There were only two radio runs in the six months involving the homeless camp and none were arrested during the period.

He walked the report to the Captain who forwarded it directly to the Chief. The fate of the program was in his hands.

# CHAPTER NINE

James sent an email to all of the participating agencies that he would be taking a two week vacation and asking them to keep up on the needs of the homeless. He and Karen decided to take a train ride to Denver for their vacation. The thirty-one hour ride would give the peace and solitude he needed to try to de-stress. He left his Cincinnati Police badge on his shirt and his gun on the belt in his closet. He wanted to be as far as possible from law enforcement.

He and Karen marveled at the beauty of the country as the train slowly chugged along. They got a berth to allow them to sleep and ate and sipped wine the whole trip. They checked into a hotel in Denver and did little other than enjoy each other's company. When they arrived back into Cincinnati, James felt like a renewed man. He was still experiencing nightmares, but they were becoming more and more sporadic.

When he returned to work, there was a message that he needed to schedule a meeting with the Chief. The message did not reveal his decision, and the anticipation of not knowing whether the program would continue was killing him. He arrived at the Chief's office and was told the Chief was waiting for him. The Chief shook his hand and told him the program would be made permanent, but that was not the reason he called James to the office. The Chief said, "I have received calls from urban police departments from all over the country asking that we provide them details of what we have done and the results. I also forwarded the complete report to the International Association of Police Chiefs and they want you to make a presentation at their annual convention in Tucson, Arizona in September. Would you be willing to do that for the department?" James had an ear-to-ear smile when he answered, "Of course I would, sir."

James was sent a schedule of appearances in Chicago, Philadelphia, Miami and Jacksonville and told he needed to create a presentation to the command staff of each agency explaining how to set up a similar program. He was also told that the IACP presentation would need to be three hours in length to be conducted twice during the conference. The IACP has over thirty-five thousand members from police agencies all over the world.

The Chief also wanted the local program expanded to each of the City's six police districts and James should work with the District commanders to set it up. The Chief approved unlimited overtime to allow James to accomplish the tasks and James would no longer report to the District Two commander, he would report to the Assistant Chief of Operations. He would also have a take home marked police vehicle.

James was sitting at his desk compiling the data for his monthly report when the radio cracked, "Car 2002 call Communications as soon as possible." James picked up the phone and punched the four digit extension and said, "This is 2002, you gave me a Signal 55." The operator said, "District one has a jumper on the Suspension bridge who asked for you by name." James jumped out of his chair and ran out of the District to his cruiser. Activating the lights and siren, he sped toward Columbia Parkway which was the shortest route to downtown. When he arrived at the bridge which runs from Covington, Kentucky into downtown Cincinnati and was the precursor to the Brooklyn Bridge, he saw a male in his thirties standing on a ledge appearing to be ready to jump into the Ohio River. James got within ten feet of the man and said, “Hey Marty, what is going on here?” Marty is the name that James knew him as from the homeless camp said, “Don’t come any closer, I will jump!” James softly answered, “You specifically asked for me man, talk to me. What is happening here?” Marty started crying and said, “Someone stole my food and my blanket. I just can’t win.” James smiled and said, “I have those items in my cruiser for you. Come down and I will give them to you now.” Marty screamed, “Get all these people out of here or I will jump!” James told a Covington cop to close off their end of the bridge and called Communications to close the Cincinnati side. Then he ordered people to get back into their cars on the bridge and to leave the area. Once all the people were off the bridge, James returned to Marty saying, “I have never lied to you Marty and I did what you wanted. Now come down and let’s talk.” Marty was appearing to have balance issues and James told him that two firemen would come to help him down. Both firefighters were tethered to a fire truck to ensure that Marty did not try to take one or both of them the one hundred foot drop to the icy river. Officer Michael Partin, a Covington, Kentucky cop fell to his death from the bridge attempting to arrest a DUI in January, 1998. His body was not recovered for several days.

The firefighters brought Marty down and handed him off to James. James told Marty, "I need to handcuff you to place you in my car by policy. I will be taking you to University of Cincinnati Medical Center to have a doctor check you out. If the doctor says you are okay, I will take you back to the camp and replace what was stolen from you.

James walked Marty into the psychiatric unit of the hospital and waited while he was interviewed by the staff who determined that he was not a threat to himself or others. James placed the cuffs back on and took Marty back to the encampment and gave him a new peanut butter, jelly and blanket. Marty thanked James profusely and walked away.

***

James was headed to the District to start his day when a call came out, "Cars 2104 and 2105, respond to the Red Bank Road entrance to I-71 south, investigate a naked female in the grass." James clicked the microphone and said, "Car 2002, give the other units a disregard, I will take that run. I am on I-71 southbound at this time." When James arrived three minutes later, there were already six cruisers at the scene because cops never want to miss craziness in action. James saw the woman, who appeared to be in her fifties, running back and forth in the grass next to the Interstate butt naked. He got out of his cruiser and walked toward her saying, "Hey Liz, you need to get some clothes on." Liz, that is the name he knew her by from the homeless camp, ignored him and continued to dance and run in the grass. James continued, "Liz, you know me and I have always been polite to you. Come over and let's talk." With that, the naked woman walked toward James and he was able to wrap her in a blanket. James thought to himself that this was likely a very pretty lady many years ago, before the alcohol rotted her brain. The other cruisers immediately left because the show was over. James placed her in the back seat of the cruiser and took her back to the homeless camp telling her, "Liz, this cannot happen because I cannot keep you out of jail if it does." He left after she put clothing on and completed the drive to the District.

# CHAPTER TEN

James received an email telling him that he was being dispatched to Philadelphia, Pennsylvania for three days to assist them in developing their CSO program.

James arrived at the airport for his flight and approached the security checkpoint. In his hand was his badge and ID card and a letter from the Police Chief stating that his trip was on official business of the Cincinnati Police Department. The TSA agent refused to accept the information to allow him pass through with his firearm, so James asked for a TSA supervisor. When the female supervisor got an attitude, James demanded that the Airport Police be called. It took about ten minutes for two cops to get there and James explained the situation to them. The two cops looked at the TSA people and told James, "Just follow us through the checkpoint and we will walk you to your gate." The three arrived at the gate and James thanked them and watched them walk away.

The flight from the Cincinnati airport, which is actually located in Kentucky took just under two hours and was uneventful. James was met at the gate by two uniformed airport cops who led him into a back area to an elevator. They told him that his luggage was being retrieved and that a Lieutenant from Philadelphia PD was waiting for him at the Airport Police office. The Lieutenant shook his hand when they arrived at the office and said, "Welcome to the City of Brotherly Love. I will take you to your hotel and then pick you up tomorrow morning."

James got checked into the Philadelphia Marriott and needed to decide what to do for dinner. The bellman told him to check out the world famous Philadelphia cheesesteak. James walked out to the cab stand and told the driver to take him to the best cheesesteak in town. The driver smiled and told him Gino's on the south side of town was the best. The driver took him past row houses with parking on both sides of the street, leaving room for only one direction of cars to move at a time. James was surprised to see the addons in metal cups outside the wall of the open air stand. He took his sandwich and fries back to the hotel and enjoyed the City's signature dish.

The next morning, he went down to the lobby for breakfast and returned to his room to dress. He brought his full uniform with him and went down to the lobby wearing it. The Lieutenant looked shocked to see him wearing a Cincinnati Police uniform, but James told him he would explain when they got into the car. James said, "I want you to see the reaction the homeless people will have when they see a cop who is not a threat to them. Just take me to a camp of your choice." The Lieutenant showed him the homeless living on the streets around downtown and then took him to an underpass where over seventy people had created a camp.

James told the Lieutenant, "Watch the facial expressions as we approach and then see how they change as we interact." James got out of the car and put on his white police hat and walked toward the group who looked confused because they did not recognize the uniform. James loudly said, "My name is Officer Daniels and I am a cop in Cincinnati, Ohio. I have no authority to arrest anyone here. I just want to talk. We have a program in Cincinnati that is designed to improve, not change, your life. Your choices are for you to make, so we offer help to let you survive the brutal conditions in which you live. The guy behind me is a Philly cop and he is here to learn what we can do to help you survive." The residents walked up close to look at his badge and police patch and their facial expressions changed radically. They opened up and talked about their needs and their fear of the police.

When the two cops got back into the cruiser, the Lieutenant said, "I have to say that it was enlightening."

The Lieutenant took James to a meeting of some of the groups that had been suggested to Philly police by the Cincinnati Chief. At the meeting were reps of Dignity and Fairness-Homeless, United Way, Philabundence, a food bank, and St. John's Hospice. James was still in uniform and got the same response from the group of attendees. He spoke to the group for just over an hour explaining how he utilized Cincinnati organizations to make his program work.

The Lieutenant was taking James back to the hotel and offered to take James to dinner. James gladly accepted and they went to Vernick's Fish located in downtown. The Lieutenant told James about the history of the restaurant and the two enjoyed the fish. James was dropped off at the hotel and would be picked up at 9am the next day to meet with the brass of the PD.

James had his uniform on again as they went to the Administration Building of the Philadelphia Police Department. In attendance in the large conference room was the Superintendent and all of the command staff. James could feel the tension in the room indicating that many really did not want to be there and had zero interest in what he was going to say.

James addressed the group with, "Ladies and gentlemen, I understand that many of you are not into foo-foo policing and neither am I. I am a Community Service Officer with the Cincinnati Police Department. In fact, I am the only CSO.I created the program and have only been a cop for a little over two years. My background was a Vice-President of a major bank where I supervised over two hundred employees and sat in a corner office on the top floor, but I wanted something more from my life. Most cops feel that dealing with homeless is beneath them. They want to go out and kick ass and take names. I had no need to get that kind of rush. I became a cop to help people and that is what instituted my program. In the last year of this program, I have arrested a bank robber and took down an active shooter at a high school. I am a real cop. I can take the garbage calls that street cops do not want and still have an impact on crime in my city." It became quickly apparent that he had piqued the interest of the room. He walked the group through the positive and problematic areas of the homeless interaction with law enforcement. Cincinnati provided a set of handouts for the Police Department to copy and give to the participants. At the end of the presentation, he opened up for questions from the group. A female Assistant Chief asked, "What would we be looking for in an officer." James answered, "A person who is less interested in arrest statistics than in helping people, but one who is not looking for a place to hibernate and draw a paycheck."

When the presentation was concluded, the Superintendent handed James a plaque with the Philadelphia PD patch and inscribed with his name.

***

James landed at the Cincinnati airport feeling like he had just run a full marathon. The trip to Philly drained all of his energy and he just wanted to get home. He walked to the baggage area and located a help phone that went directly to the Airport Police. He told the dispatcher that his cruiser was parked in their lot and asked if she would have a police unit meet him for a ride. The cruiser was waiting for him when he walked out of the terminal. The drive to the station took only about two minutes, so there was no time for anything other than pleasantries. When they arrived at his cruiser, the female officer quipped, "You might need these" and handed him the cruiser keys which he had been asked to leave in case they needed to move it. James loaded his baggage into the back seat and headed home. He wanted a home cooked meal and to be with his wife and just cruised on I-275 east back into Ohio. He would smile every time he would come up on a car on the Interstate because as soon as the driver would see him their brake lights would immediately go on. He pulled into his driveway and unloaded the baggage and walked into his house where his wife was waiting at the door. He could smell the dinner cooking and she had a big smile on her face. She told him they would eat in the family room because she had something he would want to see. When they were ready to eat, she turned on the dvr to the six o'clock news which was already cued up. The reporter was telling the viewers about the Cincinnati Police sending an officer to help the Philadelphia Police Department deal with their homeless and that their affiliate station WFIL had captured video of the officer on a tour of a homeless camp. They then cut to video of James lecturing the senior command staff of the Philadelphia PD. Lastly, they told of a letter that the Cincinnati Police Chief received from the Police Superintendent of Philadelphia thanking the CPD for the professionalism of the officer. Karen told James how proud she was of him and hugged him again.

***

James got ready for his first day back at work and decided to start his day by following up on property warnings he had issued. He arrived at the first site to see that the junk vehicles were still in the front yard. He called Communications Section and requested three tow trucks to remove the vehicles. It took over an hour for the wreckers to arrive and take the vehicles to the Police Impound Lot. When they were gone, James tacked a court summons to the front door of the house.

James went to the second location and saw the grass was still uncut. He contacted the Parks Department who told him they had a crew close by and would arrive shortly. The four person crew arrived and the supervisor told James they would need to leave and get a commercial mower because of the height of the overgrowth. They returned twenty minutes later with a mower on a trailer and started mowing. They were about halfway done when a truck pulled into the driveway, A male jumped out of the truck and began screaming at the work crew, ordering them to leave his property. James walked over to the driver and told him that he was responsible for the crew's presence and that screaming at him would not end well for the homeowner. The man told James, "I ain't paying for this, so knock yourself out." James smiled and answered, "The City will place a lien on the property and will recover the costs when you sell the house." The owner cussed as he walked into the front door of the house. When the crew left, James called Communications requesting a cover car to assist in serving a summons to the owner. Within two minutes, three police cars pulled up and James walked up to the front door of the house. He knocked on the door which flew open and James could see the rage in the man's eyes. He told the man to sign the summons and saw that the man was assessing his options, being there were now four cops in his yard. He grabbed the citation book and signed the ticket. James handed the man his copy and the guy went back into the house slamming the front door as hard as he could. James looked at the other cops and said, "Another happy camper has been serviced." The cops laughed and got back into their cruisers and left.

James walked in the rear entrance of the District and was immediately greeted by male cops bowing in reverence to royalty. Two female officers curtsied in his presence. James smiled and waved his extended middle finger at the cops walking into his office and closing the door. He spent the next two hours finalizing his report to the Police Chief about the success of the Philly PD trip and then drove to the homeless camp in the underpass and replenished their supply of peanut butter, jelly and crackers. It was a great day.

## CHAPTER ELEVEN

James was driving to a scheduled community meeting in the Mount Lookout area when the radio cracked an Officer Needs Assistance call. James activated the lights and siren and arrived in less than two minutes. As he put the car into park, James heard two gunshots ring out and called into his portable radio, "Car 2002, shots fired, repeating SHOTS FIRED!" He was at the officer's side within seconds and the officer still had his gun in his hand. There was a male on the ground with blood coming out of his chest. The officer looked at James and said, "I thought he had a gun. I thought he had a gun." James did not acknowledge the statement and ran to his cruiser to get the first aid kit. He ran back and applied pressure to the two bullet holes in the man's chest. He heard another officer request a paramedic respond. When the Rescue Unit arrived, they told James to move away and let them work on the man. It took only seconds for them to announce that the man had expired. James told the medics not to touch anything and to move away to save the scene for the homicide investigators. James told two cops to take the officer's gun and get him away from other cops. He said, "He has rights and we need to make sure that he gets them." A Lieutenant arrived at the scene and immediately told James to drive down to the Homicide Unit to be interviewed.

James made the drive to downtown and was greeted by two burly old cops. Bob Sendel had twenty-seven years on the job and Roger Wilde had thirty-one years. The two old dicks took James back into an interview room and had him recount what he saw and heard from the time he arrived until the time he left. When he was finished, Sendel asked, "Another officer told us that the officer told you 'I thought he had a gun.' That was not in the statement you just made. Is the other officer lying?" "It was not in my statement because I did not hear anything at that time. That does not mean that it was not said, my total focus was on the male who had been shot. Did you ask the officer if I responded to the statement?" "The officer said you did not." "Well, isn't that something to which a response would be likely if I had actually heard it?"

Wilde reached under the table and de-activated the audio and video recording. James watched as the light on the camera turned off. Wilde looked at James and said, "I think you heard every word that was said and just want to protect another cop. The fact that you did not respond gave you plausible deniability which is difficult to disprove, but I am sure you heard it." James glared at the old cop and said, "Are we done here? Some of us actually have to work for a living." When James arrived back at his cruiser, he immediately signed-off from the in-car computer and drove home.

When Karen opened the front door, she could immediately smell the aromas of a special dinner. She followed the smell into the kitchen and passed the table with a tablecloth and a lit single candle in the center. She saw James at the stove hovering over his masterpiece. She walked up to him and kissed him on the cheek whispering, "Someone has something to confess."

"I responded to an officer involved shooting and may have fibbed into the investigators." When she asked why he felt it necessary to do that James said. "Because I don't know what caused him to believe that the guy had a gun, but I am not going to jam him up for something said in the heat of the moment. My response did not hurt or help him and others apparently heard his response and will testify to it. I hope nothing comes of it, but I don't know."

Three days later the evening news announced that the officer had been indicted by a Grand Jury on a charge of Negligent Homicide, a misdemeanor under Ohio law. James was notified that he would be called as a prosecution witness in the case.

James testified at the officer's trial with the same story he had given the whole way through. The prosecutor assigned to the case asked about the testimony from the other officer about the cop's statement. James answered, "I have consistently said that I do not challenge that the officer did or did not make the statement. I only stated that I did not hear it." The young prosecutor said, "And you conveniently did not respond to the defendant's statement." James shot back, "Excuse me? Are you calling me a liar?" The prosecutor "I am only saying that your testimony is really convenient, officer. No further questions." There was an immediate rush of media hounds as James walked out of the Courthouse yelling questions. His police car was surrounded with cameras and microphones with one moron standing inches from the front bumper. James activated the overhead lights and tapped the siren and slowly inched forward, causing the media hound to move out of the way. After a two day trial before a judge, the officer was found not guilty.

James was in his office typing a report for a Community Council meeting when his office line rang. It was a call from the Chief's office telling him to report to the Prosecutor's office. James left the office confused over what the prosecutor would want. When he arrived, he was told that the County Prosecutor was waiting for him and he was led into his office. The prosecutor shook his hand and said, "I have been made aware that there was a problem with one of my Assistant's yesterday. What he said was out of bounds and he has been suspended and will be transferred back into the Juvenile Division. I know that you took it as a personal affront and I am hoping that my action today will be seen as a sign that this office supports our police." James said, "I dislike my character being assassinated for no valid reason. He is allowed his personal opinion, but to express it in open court with no evidence to back it up is reckless. I try not to hold grudges, but this really hurt." The prosecutor said, "If you want his head on a plate, I can do that. The reason that I immediately took your side is the way you responded to a challenge you could not anticipate. That shows your commitment to the truth. If my move satisfies you, then he does not lose his job and we can all move on."

The two men shook hands and James returned to work.

***

It was three o'clock in the morning and James was sleeping when his city cell phone rang. The male voice on the other end said, “This is Captain Kellogg and I am the night chief. The Chief wants you to respond to Loveland-Madeira Road and meet Loveland Police who have a vehicle stopped containing two of our cops who are intoxicated. The Chief wants you to tell the female Captain that her police powers are suspended and to take the firearms from both of the officers. You are to deliver both weapons to the Chief. If you have any problems, call me immediately and I will resolve them.”

James dressed and drove to the location where he saw two Loveland cop cars parked behind a white Toyota Camry. He was told that the Loveland cops would be arresting the Captain for D.U.I. and that her Lieutenant husband was being really mouthy. He approached the female, who was being very cooperative, and told her he needed her badge and gun and that her police powers were being temporarily suspended. She told James that her firearm was in her purse which was in the Loveland police car and handed him her badge case. Her husband was standing outside of the passenger side of the Camry screaming at the Loveland cops. James walked up to him and said, “The Police Chief has ordered me to take control of your firearm. You can go to the Chief’s office and retrieve it in the morning. The Lieutenant responded. “You don’t outrank me, get the fuck out of my face.”

James took a step back and called the number given to him by the night chief who said, “Hand the moron the phone and tell him I want to talk to him.” James handed the phone to the Lieutenant saying, “The night chief wants to talk to you.” The night chief said, “I do outrank you and if I have to come there and get your weapon, I will also be taking your badge and I will fire your ass. This officer is operating under the direct authority of the Police Chief. Am I making my perfectly clear?" The Lieutenant softly answered 'Yes, sir" and the night chief hung up on him. He removed his .40 caliber handgun from his belt and handed it to James, who immediately removed the magazine of ammunition and cleared the bullet in the chamber and placed all of it into an evidence bag. James did the same thing with the weapon from the Captain's purse and got back into his cruiser and returned home. James called the night chief and told him that both officers had complied and that the Captain was being arrested and her husband was told to walk home because he was too intoxicated to drive.

James sat at his kitchen table and made coffee because his heart was beating at a mile per minute. He knew that there was no way that he would be getting back to sleep. Just after five a.m. he got into his cruiser and made the drive to District One headquarters. He walked into the front entrance and the desk officer immediately hit the release to open the entry door into the station. James laid the two evidence bags on the desk and told the officer, "These need to get to the Chief's Office first thing in the morning." The desk cop shrugged his shoulders and moved the envelopes to the rear of the desk. James laid a form on the desk which was titled "Chain of Custody" and told the desk cop, "Sign this," knowing that the form made the desk cop responsible for the envelopes. The desk cop looked really pissed as he signed the form and James returned to his car and headed for his office.

James was getting ready to make his morning welfare checks when the phone in his office rang. The male on the other end said, "My name is Detective Douglas from the Metro Nashville Police Department. I wanted to notify you personally that your daughter Kelly is in the Vanderbilt University Medical Center after suffering serious injuries from a domestic with her boyfriend. We are searching for him now. She was assaulted in her dorm room and is expected to need surgery for facial and other injuries to her body." There was a pause after which James said, "My wife and I will be in Nashville in about six hours as I have to go home first. Thank you for the call, I really appreciate it."

James went into the Captain's office and told her that he needed a few days of emergency leave and relayed what the Nashville cop told him. The Captain told him, "Take as long as you need, we will cover for you here. When he got into his cruiser to go home, he called his wife at her work and told her to go home and he would meet her there. He only told her Kelly was in the hospital and they needed to go to Nashville.

He arrived home first and threw some clothes into a suitcase. When Karen got home, she packed her suitcase and threw some snacks into a bag for the two hundred and thirty mile drive. James was breaking every speed law and made it to just south of Louisville, Kentucky before he saw blue lights flashing behind him. The trooper walked up to the driver's side of the car when James hung his badge case out of the window. James told the trooper, "I know I was speeding and am sorry. My eighteen year old daughter was assaulted by her boyfriend and Nashville P.D. told me she was going into surgery." The trooper looked into the car and said, "Drive safe and best wishes for her recovery," then turned and walked back to his cruiser. James put the car into drive and sped away.

When they arrived at the hospital, they ran into the main entrance and asked where surgeries were performed. They followed the directions to the fifth floor and stopped at the nurse's desk to find their daughter. The nurse told them, "Your daughter went into surgery less than one hour ago with significant injuries. You can wait in the surgical waiting area which is the third door to your left."

James and Karen walked to the waiting room and saw a man sitting in the room. When they sat down, the man wearing a suit walked up to them and said, "I am Dave Douglas with the Metro Nashville Police Department. I wanted to be here when you arrived. I have not yet talked to your daughter as she was taken into surgery just before I arrived. We just captured the boyfriend and I am going to the station to talk to him. You can come with me if you would like and your wife can call when your daughter gets out of surgery. Karen nodded her head that James should accept the offer and the two walked out the door.

When they arrived at the central building of Nashville P.D. Det. Douglas said, "I hope you are able to control your emotions when you see him. I know that, if it were my daughter, I would want to kill him." James assured the cop that he would remain professional. The Detective took James to a room with a one way mirror where he could watch and hear the interrogation and Douglas walked into the room where the suspect was in handcuffs seated in a chair. After reading the suspect his rights, the detective opened softly with, "I understand that people lose their temper with a girlfriend and things can escalate quickly. I would like to get your side of the story. Otherwise, I will have to charge you with multiple felonies carrying a lot of years in prison."

The twenty year old boy said, "I didn't do nothing to her. I don't understand what you are talking about." The detective laughed and said, "That is not what people on her dorm floor told me and you should have waved at the camera in the hallway that has you going in and out of her dorm room. It also shows blood on your shirt when you rode the elevator down to leave. The day of bullshit was yesterday. That help jog your memory dude?"

James stood at the mirror seething as he listened to the man lie to the police. He was surprised when he saw Douglas waving him into the Interrogation Room and walked to the next room. When he entered the young man looked up and said, "Rutro, must be good cop, bad cop time." James looked at the kid with a scowl that would kill and Douglas said, "I want you to meet her father, a cop from Cincinnati, Ohio." James sat down in a chair and said, "Believe me, I will follow you through every step of the court process and work hard to make sure you spend the majority of your life in a prison cell. Only a punk beats up a woman and I would like to understand what set you off." The suspect looked at Douglas and said, "I think I want a lawyer now" and the interrogation ended. The suspect was taken out of the room by two uniformed officers and

Douglas said, “That went well. I will keep you in the loop as I will be filing felony assault and domestic violence charges today. I will take you back to the hospital now. We have an arrangement with a hotel near the hospital where we house guest instructors. I will take care of getting you a room there.”

When they arrived at the hospital, James shook the detective’s hand and said, “Thank you for the professional courtesy. I will forever be in your debt.” James went back to the waiting room where Karen was sitting with her head in her hands. She told James that Kelly was still in surgery and that a doctor came in and told her the injuries were not life threatening.

They sat in the waiting room for another two hours when the door opened and a surgeon came in. He told them, “Your daughter is out of surgery and is in recovery now. The reason that we opened her up was that one of her fractured ribs was very close to penetrating her heart and she was suffering internal bleeding from her injuries. We were able to stop the bleeding and reset her ribs back into place. We are going to keep her for a couple of days to monitor her progress. Why don’t you go out for dinner and come back when we move her to a private room? Any questions you have for me before I leave?” He waited silently for a minute and then left the room.

James and his wife drove to the hotel that was reserved for them. James called Douglas and invited him to join them for dinner saying, “You can introduce us to Nashville cuisine.” The Detective laughed and said he would come to the hotel and pick them up. He took them to a restaurant a few miles away and ordered them Hot Nashville chicken and French fries. They ate and talked about the similarities and differences in policing in their urban cities. Nashville is a metropolitan police department having jurisdiction anywhere within the county, while Cincinnati is limited to the city boundaries. When they were done, the detective returned the couple to their hotel and told them he would keep them up on the progress in the case and to call him when Kelly was up for an interview.

They returned to the hospital and found out Kelly has just gotten into her hospital room. Karen gasped when she saw the injuries to Kelly's face, grabbing James by the arm. Kelly was sedated and the nurse said there was no reason for them to stay as Kelly would be out for the night.

They returned to the hotel and went to bed.

***

They arrived at the hospital early the next morning and were told by a nurse that Kelly had awakened and to come back after lunch to spend time with her. They returned just after noon and Kelly had an ear-to-ear smile when they walked into the room. Her voice was weak, but that was to be expected after all she had been through. They did not want to stay long as it would wear Kelly out. After they left James called the detective to tell him that Kelly was available for an interview.

At lunch Karen suggested that James return home and she would fly home after Kelly got back to normal. After a heated discussion, James agreed to drive back to Cincinnati the next day.

## CHAPTER TWELVE

James finished his morning paperwork and drove to the homeless camp for a welfare check. He had to wear a mask and gloves due to a virus paralyzing the nation. As soon as he arrived, he was approached by a man who told him about a woman resident being sick. James walked back and found the woman shivering under a blanket even though it was eighty degrees outside. James got on the radio and requesting a rescue unit and stayed with the woman until the paramedics arrived. He was surprised to see the medics wearing hazardous materials suits from head-to-toe. They loaded the woman onto the gurney and, as they were leaving, one of the medics looked at James and said, "Thanks pal, now we are going to have to disinfect the whole rig again."

James was sitting in his cruiser when the radio cracked, "Attention all cars, all departments, OSP in pursuit of a semi with a trailer. Pursuit just turned onto southbound I-71 from eastbound I-275." James drove onto the southbound entrance ramp on I-71 waiting for the chase when the radio cracked again, "Attention all cars, all departments, Ohio Highway Patrol cruiser involved in a crash southbound I-71 at Red Bank Road. James now had a dilemma as the crash was less than two miles away, but the semi would be passing him momentarily. James quickly decided that the injured officer was his priority and drove across the southbound lanes into the median to get onto northbound.

When he arrived at the crash, he could see a badly damaged cruiser and two troopers working on the officer laying in the grass. As he got closer, he saw that the injured officer was his neighbor. A state patrol cruiser pulled up and a Lieutenant started walking toward the injured officer. James ran up to the Lieutenant and said, "Lieutenant, Dave Bristol is my neighbor and a friend who we have dinners with. Let me tell her about her husband as she is going to be more comfortable with me than another trooper." The supervisor thought for a moment and nodded in agreement.

James jumped into his cruiser and activated the lights and siren. While driving he called his wife at her work and told her about the crash. As he was arriving at his street, he turned off both the lights and the siren and pulled into Dave's driveway. He rang the doorbell and, when Dave's wife opened the door, she smiled and told James that Dave was not home. James told her, "I already know that. Dave was involved in a traffic crash on Interstate 71 and I am here to take you to the hospital. She quickly turned and left the door open while retrieved her purse and keys.

They got into James' police car and James drove out of the neighborhood. As soon as they reached the main street, James hit the overhead lights and the siren and drove to the University of Cincinnati Medical Center. He parked in the circle at the front entrance of the hospital where they could see several officers from Ohio Highway Patrol, Cincinnati, Hamilton County Sheriff and University of Cincinnati milling around. The two entered the front door and were immediately approached by the State Police

Lieutenant who softly said. “I am truly sorry, but Dave did not get to the hospital in time to save him. He passed away about twenty minutes ago.” James grabbed the woman whose legs had buckled out and held her close as she sobbed uncontrollably. James could see tears in the faces of the other cops in the area, but this was not the time for him to cry.

James had to almost carry her back to his cruiser. He called Karen and told her the bad news. She said she would meet them at Dave’s home. When the two arrived at Dave’s home, there were already two Highway Patrol vehicles parked in front. One had the chaplain of the Patrol and the other was a Captain from Dave’s post. The three men provided support to help her get into the house where Karen was waiting at the front door. James was moved by the fact that the whole neighborhood was out in their front yards with signs of prayers for her loss. Neighbors began arriving with food for the people sitting with her and offering condolences.

They had been at the home less than two hours when the door opened and the Ohio Governor walked in. He dropped to one knee and told her that the State’s flags had been lowered to half-staff out of respect for Dave’s service and that his office would make sure that her needs were filled. There were tears visible in the Governor’s eyes as he talked with the wife. He and his security detail left about an hour later.

There were media vans clogging the street and James put in a call to the County Sheriff to get them moved. A deputy arrived and ordered all of the media hounds to park somewhere out or he would tow all of the media trucks for blocking a fire lane.

James was mildly surprised when the President of the Cincinnati F.O.P walked into the house. He told Dave's wife that her loss was also a loss to all Cincinnati Police officers and that the F.O.P. would be providing an honor guard to show their respect. Karen did everything she could to help the woman cope with the overwhelming outpouring of support from the law enforcement community.

***

The Ohio Highway Patrol made all of the arrangements for the funeral service, but made the exception of allowing James to be a pall bearer. At the layout there were over one thousand police officers from all over the nation waiting in line to pay their respect to the fallen officer. Karen and James stood on either side of the widow to help her keep some composure. James was in his police uniform and told the widow what agency the individual officer represented. Forty-six of the fifty state police agencies sent a cruiser to participate in the service. The three hour viewing time went into seven hours and the widow was physically and mentally drained.

The funeral service was at the Methodist church the family attended. Every seat was full and uniformed officers were lined against three walls. The overflow stood in line in the parking lot and the line of police vehicles stretched almost a mile long.

Wives of Ohio troopers were also present every step of the way because they understood that someday it might be them placed in that position.

It was a long day for everyone. The service lasted more than two hours and the procession took another hour to drive the one and one-half miles from the church to the cemetery. James was allowed to lead the procession and passed hundreds of people lining the streets waving American flags and Back the Blue flags. People brought their children who placed their hands over their heart as the hearse passed by and fire trucks lined the route with their ladders crossed and American flags hanging down to pay tribute to a hero. The Governor sent a message which was broadcast over loud speaker to the almost two thousand attendees. The Hamilton County Sheriff provided their bagpipes and OSP provided a twenty-one gun salute as a send-off to a fallen brother.

When the procession arrived at the cemetery, James was impressed by the hundreds of uniformed cops from all over the country and around the world standing at attention and saluting as the hearse passed.

The Ohio Patrol broadcast the officer's final call followed by the playing of Taps and a twenty-one gun salute. James was moved to the core.

Loveland Police got the use of a rental lodge and the F.O.P. provided food for all that wanted to attend. Karen took the widow home while James thanked everyone he could on behalf of the widow.

# CHAPTER THIRTEEN

James was having major difficulty handling the loss of his neighbor and friend.  He sat at the dining room table with his wife and talked about being fifty-seven years old and in fear that he was getting too old to play policeman any longer. He told her that he was considering taking the Lieutenant's examination because it would take him off the streets and reduce the risks of the job.

James was deeply disappointed when he saw that he finished third on the test. There was only one vacancy to be filled and the promotion list would expire in two years. There are relatively few vacancies at the Lieutenant level and above.

Three months passed and James was in his office when he received a call from the Chief's secretary telling him to report to the Chief's office immediately. It was a long drive downtown as James mulled over what he could have done wrong to get the Chief's attention. When he walked into the office, the secretary had no smile on her face as she pointed toward the Chief's door. James walked into the office with his white hat under his left arm and immediately sat down in the chair that the Chief pointed to. His nerves were running wild.

Without looking up, the Chief said, "I received retirement papers from two Captains today, and you will be getting promoted within the next two weeks. After all you have done for this department in your time here, I thought it only fair that I give you your choice of assignments as a

Lieutenant. I do not need an answer today, but you need to decide within the next few days. Congratulations on your promotion Lieutenant. The drive back to his office was a blur as James thought about what he wanted to do in his future with the police department.

James took his wife to the country club for a special dinner and they kicked around his options as to his new assignment. James called the Chief and told him he had made a decision. He wanted to be in charge of the Recruiting Unit where he could help mold the future of the department by finding the best available candidates.

***

Both of his children returned to Cincinnati to attend the promotion ceremony which was held in City Council chambers. Local television crews were present to capture the moment for the evening news. His daughter was now a Nurse Practitioner working at Vanderbilt University Medical Center and his son was working for a law firm as a Litigation Specialist in Dallas, Texas. Both were still single and Karen told them both she wanted grandchildren while she was still young enough to enjoy them.

***

James reported to his new position and met the people who would be working for him. There were two recruiting officers, three background investigators and a secretary. They would work out of offices at the Police Academy. One of the recruiting cops was an African-American female by the name of Doris Pope. The other was an Asian Male named Kim Jung Xang. Both showed great personalities and wore the uniform with dignity and respect. The three investigators all had years of experience and wanted only the best to continue the traditions of the Cincinnati Police.

James met with the two recruiters and they designed a plan to make appearances at all of the colleges in the Cincinnati area and locate hiring events as well.

James developed a program to lure qualified candidates to the Cincinnati Police Department. He sent the two recruiters to Minneapolis, Minnesota to a hotel and the Fraternal Order of Police and put out a press release to local media that Cincinnati, Ohio would be taking applications. The response from the Minnesota law enforcement community was overwhelming. They had forty-two men and women show up at the hotel expressing interest. As a result, James sent a polygraph operator and the investigators for background checks. He also convinced the Civil Service Commission to send a testing team to Minneapolis to administer the written test.

After this success, James turned his attention to the State of Washington, first in Seattle and then in Portland. Both cities had inherent problems between the Police Department and the politicians and line cops were eager to find an alternative.

The last stop on the road trip was in New York. New York where the Mayor had disparaged the Police Department and cut funding.

The road trip got enough qualified candidates to fill a recruit class of sixty cops. The working experience level spanned less than one year to more than fifteen and included officers with investigative and supervisory experience.

***

James stayed in the office while his staff was on the road. He received a call from the Chief's office telling him the new Police Chief wanted to meet with him. When he walked into the office, the secretary smiled at him and told him the Chief was waiting for him. Dave Ballford had been the Assistant Chief in charge of the Patrol Division when he was appointed Chief. James had never met him but knew that the street cops loved him because he supported them, even when the politicians did not.

The Chief pointed to a chair and James sat down. The Chief said, "Although we have never met, I have followed your career. I must tell you that I am impressed with what you have done for the Police Department. Even though you got a very late start. I am looking to have two recruit classes in the next two years, and I expect you to fill the seats with qualified candidates. The city is interested in the diversity of each class, while I want the best people who want to serve the people of this city. I know that your team has gone to cities that failed to support their cops and that is a great idea. I hope that it bears fruit. Anything this office can do to support your effort only requires a call.

As he drove back to his office, James had an ear-to-ear smile. He felt that his work had been recognized and that he had the support of the new administration.

# CHAPTER FOURTEEN

James was helping wash the dinner dishes when he heard the doorbell ring. He saw two men standing on the porch as he walked to the door. One was wearing a suit and tie and the other was casually dressed. When he opened the door, the man in the suit said, "My name is Walter Kennedy and I am the Mayor of the City of Loveland. With me is Don Sizemore and he is our Safety Director. May we come in and chat?

James stepped aside and watched the two men walk toward the family room. As he passed the kitchen, he motioned Karen to follow. The four sat down and the Mayor said, "Our Police Chief just announced his intention to retire next month and we are looking for a successor. We came here to offer you the position. Two of our recent Chiefs came from the leadership ranks of the Cincinnati Police and you have long standing ties to this community. We are aware of the things that you have accomplished in Cincinnati and think that you would bring a skillset that fits the needs of our city. If you are not interested, we will advertise the position. You are the only person we have contacted so far.

James glanced over at his wife who was nodding her approval. He looked the two men directly in the eye and said, "Of course I am interested." The mayor said, "We are not the final decision makers in this. You will have to sit and be interviewed by the entire City Council who will vote on your appointment. This will be a private meeting because personnel issues are not subject to the Sunshine Law. It will be next Tuesday evening if that works for your schedule. The two men rose from their chairs and shook James' hand and then left.

After they were gone, James asked Karen for her thoughts on this development. She told him that he earned this opportunity and he would be foolish to forgo the chance.

***

The two walked into the Council chambers which was empty except for the elected officials and the City Manager and Safety Director. The mayor introduced James to the elected officials and asked James if he would like to address the Council.

James had practiced his statement with his wife and incorporated the changes she suggested. He told the Council about the accomplishments he had with the homeless in Cincinnati and how he always worked to improve the relationships between the Police and the people they serve. He told the group about his understanding of the business world and how he wanted to spend the available dollars on programs that make the community safer and more viable. He emphasized the fact that he had been a resident of Loveland for over thirty years and his family's ties to the community.

When he finished, the floor opened to questions from the members of City Council. A female asked, "What changes, if any, would you immediately institute as Police Chief." James smiled and replied, "I come from an urban police department where the citizens don't know their cops and the cops don't know the people. That is different from this city and this police department. This police department is known throughout the area for its professionalism and I would need to determine how things have been done here for decades. I would not be making any changes until I have that information."

After the questions, James walked out of the chamber and immediately got a big hug from his wife who said, "You killed it!"

***

James went into the office like a regular day because he had no information as to when a decision would be made. It was just after ten o'clock when Karen called to tell him that a uniformed Loveland Police Officer had just delivered a sealed envelope to the house. James told her to open it and it said, "We would like to extend an offer of employment to you as the Police Chief for the City of Loveland, Ohio at a starting annual salary of one hundred and two thousand dollars. If you decide to accept, you will need to go to the City's doctor to pass the physical and then to Gall's Uniform Company to be fitted for your new uniform. Your badge and firearm will be provided at your swearing-in at the next regularly scheduled City Council meeting."

James would also need to write his resignation letter to Cincinnati and that would be an emotional event. After the fourth draft, James began getting frustrated because the words lacked the love that he felt for the time he had been a Cincinnati cop and he needed to decide who would be the recipient. He finally chose his direct supervisor, the Capitan who commanded the Police Academy. He wanted to thank the long list of people who helped him be successful in the job, but did not want the paper to read like *WAR AND PEACE*. He went far as to move the floor shredder next to him to make it easy to toss the drafts.

He finally came up with a one page letter which said. "This document will serve as my resignation from the Cincinnati Police Department to accept a leadership position with another law enforcement agency. It is with a heavy heart that I leave a place that has allowed me the freedom to make decisions on the service provided to the community. I will never be able to pay that debt, but I will carry it with me in the provision of police service for the remainder of my career."

He hand-delivered the letter to the Captain who appeared saddened by his decision, but said he would send it up the chain of command to the Chief of Police.

Next, he called the medical doctor the city named and scheduled his appointment for the physical for the following afternoon. When he completed his day at work, he drove to the uniform store which was just outside the downtown area and got fitted for his shirts, pants and duty belt. He was told they would be ready for him in a week.

He gave Cincinnati two weeks of notice to allow him time to get his affairs in order and assist in the transition of his position to his replacement. He also called a staff meeting of all of the people under his command to tell them in person of his upcoming departure. He felt he owed them that.

James told the recruiters and background investigators how much he appreciated their dedication and service and how much he would miss them, but this was an offer which he could not turn down. He would soon be the Police Chief of the City where he had lived for almost thirty years. The meeting ended with hugs and a few tears with everyone telling him what a great boss he was.

***

Karen called the kids to invite them to the swearing-in. Kelly and her husband would be coming with their newborn daughter from Nashville.  Dennis had a major civil trial starting and would be unable to get away.

James dressed in his new uniform for the Council meeting. He had to go to the Police Department to pick up his .40 caliber Glock semi-automatic handgun so that he would not look like a fool with an empty holster. The Council chamber was filled with people when James walked in and he stood in the back of the Chamber until they announced his appointment. He walked to the front and had his new badge pinned on his chest by the mayor, who welcomed him into the City of Loveland family. That was followed by a round of applause by the gallery.

After the swearing-in, the family went home so James could change clothes and they all went to the country club for a celebration dinner.

# CHAPTER FIFTEEN

James had his wife drive him to the police station for his first day because he would be picking up his new unmarked vehicle. When they arrived, the Safety Director and Lt. Dawn Deacon, the next highest ranking officer, were waiting at the front entrance. After introductions, they took him on a tour of the Public Safety Center which housed the police, fire, ems and 9-1-1 center. James was told that the center was under the direction of the Fire Chief.

They showed him the public entrance and Sally Walters, the Police Clerk who served at the secretary to the whole department. He saw the investigation bureau where two investigators were at their desk filling out paperwork. They only stopped for a moment to be introduced to their new boss.

When they arrived at his new office, the two wished him well and left him alone, telling him they would return to take him to lunch. James sat quietly at his new desk for a moment and then started reading the existing procedure manual. He used the intercom call Sally and told her to locate Lt. Deacon and have her come to the office. When she arrived, James told her he wanted a staff meeting with all of the supervisors for the next morning. Then he told her to schedule two meetings for the rest of the officers the following morning, leaving supervisors to answer calls for service.

When Lt. Deacon left the officer, James called Sally in and told her that he wanted to see the activity sheets from all the officers and the reports from the previous day on his desk at eight o'clock in the morning.

***

The four sergeants and the one lieutenant were seated around the conference table when James arrived. He could see the nervousness of what the new boss was going to tell them and wanted to put them at ease early on. He said, "I came from a much larger agency and understand that there are not the resources here than what we had in Cincinnati. I understand that this is a community where the officers get to personally know the residents and can tailor the service we provide to their needs. I will not be changing anything that you do until I actually understand what works for this community. I also will not be making any decisions for the foreseeable future, so any decisions that need to be will be made by Lt. Deacon. Over the next several weeks, I will be reading every policy and procedure to familiarize myself with what makes this department successful. I am here to learn from you." James related the same information to the other cops in their meeting.

***

James spent the first two weeks of the new job reading the policy and procedure manual line by line in the mornings and then riding around the City learning the streets. His morning would begin with reading the activity log of each officer and the reports generated from the previous day. He would then return the folder to Sally so that she could file them. When he was riding around the city, he would listen to the police radio traffic, but chose not to respond to any request for police service because he did not want the officers to feel like he was spying on them. After he had read the manual, James decided to actually watch the officers perform their function by riding with each for a shift. He started with the third shift which ran overnight from eleven until seven in the morning. His first partner was an eleven year veteran named Daniel Walton. The two got into the cruiser at the start of the shift and Walton was visibly uncomfortable with the position that he found himself. James started the conversation with, "I cannot lead a department that I do not understand. I want to make this a great place to live, work and play and provide a working environment that is conducive to productivity. I am not interested in how many tickets cops write; I want them to be quality tickets. I also don't care how many arrests are made; I want them to be quality arrests. I am here to learn, not manage, so I will not be making decisions on what you do or how you do it. I am here to provide you whatever support you may need. Now let's go out and serve the public."

Their first call was to assist neighboring Miami Township Police with a barricaded person in a residence. When the two arrived, they saw cruisers from Miami Township, Clermont County Sheriff and another Loveland car. A Miami Township Sergeant approached and looked directly at the Chief asking, "Can I get your cars to cover the rear side of the residence?" James smiled and looked at Walton, asking him, "is that okay with you?"

Both Loveland cars were covering the rear of the house when a call of a robbery in progress at the Speedway on Wards corner road came out over the air. Walton looked at the Chief who said, "Not my decision, do what you think is right." Walton called the Miami Township Sergeant telling him of the emergency in Loveland and the two cars had to leave. As soon as the replacement cars arrived, the Loveland cars sped off. The Loveland canine unit had already arrived and started a track of the suspects who had run into a wooded area in the rear of the business. James could tell by the aggressiveness of the dog that he had picked up a scent. They reached a creek and the dog was going crazy. The handler announced, "Come out with your hands where we can see them or I will send in the dog. You might not like the outcome if the dog comes in to find you." When no one came out, the handler issued the command, "Ajax, seek." Moments later there was screaming coming from the wooded area and the cops ran in finding the canine shredding the man's left arm. The handler called the dog off and Walton handcuffed the prisoner. James was impressed by the professional actions he had just seen.

It took three weeks to get through all of the ride-alongs and James would later tell people that he learned immensely from each and every officer.

***

Most days James would go home for lunch since he lived in the city. He would pick up the mail and eat a sandwich on the couch. He looked at the day's mail and saw an envelope marked SUMMONS. He opened the envelope to see that he was ordered to jury duty in Hamilton County for two weeks. The summons ordered him to report to the Jury Commissioner's Office inside the Hamilton County Courthouse Room 455 at nine-thirty on Monday.

***

James drove downtown and parked his unmarked car in a private parking lot. He placed his handgun in the trunk and walked the one block to the courthouse, entering through the employee entrance so he could avoid the metal detectors that the public had to pass through before entering. He dressed in a suit and tie because being in uniform was not an option.

James checked in at the reception desk and found a chair to relax and await instructions on what came next. The jury commissioner came to a podium at ten-thirty welcoming all of the people in the two rooms. He watched a video of what would be happening in the coming hours and days as a juror. He heard his name called with the second group and was told to break for lunch. They would be escorted to the courtroom in a single file based upon their assigned number. The first twelve would start the process as the potential seated jury and, if excused for cause or preemptory challenge, the next number would be moved up until the jury and alternates are chosen.

The first case which James was chosen was a civil action involving a bank being sued by a man. When the judge announced the parties and their counsel, James raised his hand and told the judge that he worked for that bank for fifteen years. He was excused from the jury pool and returned to the jury commissioner, where he was told to go home for the day.

The second day got him picked for a criminal Murder trial. When he was questioned by the defense attorney about his employment, James was excused following a pre-emptory challenge.

The third day of jury duty proved to be the charm as he was picked to sit on a civil case filed by a couple against a medical practice and two doctors for medical malpractice and wrongful death of an unborn child. The case lasted four and one-half days with expert witnesses testifying on both sides. When the jury was given the case, the eight men and four women named James their foreperson. James immediately called for a vote which was eleven to one for the defendants. James asked the one woman who voted for a finding for the plaintiff for her rationale, she was unable to explain her reasons. The other members of the jury explained their reasons for their finding and the second vote was unanimous for the defendants. The deliberations took all of fifteen minutes. James notified the bailiff that a verdict had been reached, and the verdict was read in open court.

The jurors were returned to the jury room where the attorneys involved in the case were able to ask questions. The plaintiff's attorney asked how the jury could possibly reach a decision in such a short period of time, the jury members looked to James to provide an answer.

James said, "Your clients called the doctor on Sunday morning and were told to go directly to the hospital.

Instead of doing that, they stayed at home so they could watch the Cincinnati Bengals game on television. After the game was over, they went to the hospital and the baby was delivered with the cord wrapped around its neck causing strangulation. Had they gone immediately to the hospital, as directed, they might well have saved their baby." The attorney stormed out of the room.

## CHAPTER SIXTEEN

James put all of his concentration into writing new policies and revising some of the existing ones. He would present the proposed policies to the supervisors at their staff meeting each week and give a week for them to read and digest them and offer feedback. He knew that they would make their subordinates aware of the proposals and get their input over the week, He did this so there would not be an opportunity for the rank-and-file to claim they had been sandbagged.

One proposal did cause rancor among the troops. It required all patrol officers working between the hours of eight in the morning and ten at night to initiate a single contact with a resident and a business owner every shift. The officer would ask questions from a form which would be turned in at the end of the shift. Sally would enter the responses into the computer and place them on his desk for review the next morning.

One of the first forms James reviewed had a complaint from a female resident about a house on Maple Street which had a constant flow of traffic at all hours. She told the officer that the vehicles would only stay about fifteen minutes and she believed the residents were selling drugs.

James ordered the two detectives to set up surveillance on the house to verify the information. After two day the cops reported that an unusual amount of traffic was flowing in and out of the house throughout the night. James ordered a patrol car to be nearby and make traffic stops on vehicles leaving the house to identify the occupants of the cars. The stops resulted in several arrests of people with open warrants and identified a number of persons with prior drug convictions. All of the information was presented to a judge who issued a warrant to search the premises.

The warrant was served by the countywide S.W.A.T team and drugs, money and guns were seized. The residents of the house were arrested for trafficking in narcotics and the County Prosecutor seized the house and property using a state asset forfeiture law. A judge returned the house to the owner who claimed that he had no knowledge of the activity and only rented the property to the people arrested. The judge told the owner that any subsequent violation would result in the house and property being seized as he would be outside of the "innocent owner exception" since he was now forewarned.

The bust made all four of the local television stations news broadcasts and the City Administration received multiple calls from residents thanking the police department for their efforts.

***

The second issue that was presented was more problematic. A woman reported reckless operators in her subdivision between two and four in the afternoon. James ordered the Sergeant to assign a patrol unit to the subdivision and to write citations for all violations observed. In the next two days fourteen traffic citations were issued for speeding, reckless driving and running stop signs. James was in his office when the intercom sounded.

Sally said, "Chief, there is a woman on line one wanting to lodge a complaint." James picked up the phone and the woman said, "I just a ticket from one of your cops and I was not speeding. In fact, I am the one who reported reckless drivers in the subdivision, and I got a ticket. I want it cancelled." James asked, "did the officer treat you with respect?" The woman answered, "Yes, but I was not speeding." With a wry smile James said, "Whether you were speeding or not is for a court to determine. Ohio law prohibits me from voiding a traffic citation unless another is written to replace it. You can get an attorney and plead not guilty in court and the court will determine whether or not you are guilty." He heard a click and a dial tone and hung up the phone saying, "Another satisfied customer." Several hours later James received a call from a City Council member whose sixteen year old son had received a ticket in the same subdivision. He told the man the same thing and the council member hung up on him.

## CHAPTER SEVENTEEN

James received his six month review from the Safety Director in the mail. It said:

> In the first six months of your service as Police Chief, the city has received numerous calls and letters applauding the actions of the Police Department to keep our residents safe. Job Well Done, keep it up."

James posted the letter on the bulletin board for all to see.

***

James walked into the station for the start of his day when Sally motioned him over. She told him that a man and woman were waiting in the lobby to see him about a complaint. James smiled and told Sally to give him three minutes to get his coffee and then bring them to his office.

When the door opened, James got up out of his chair and pointed to two chairs for them to sit. The male of the couple said, "No thanks, we will stand." James sat in his chair and asked, "How can I help you?" The female said, "Three nights ago my car broke down on Miamiville Road around two in the morning. About fifteen minutes later, a police car pulled in behind me and turned on the blue lights. The officer came up and offered to call a tow truck for me. When it arrived, he offered to drive me home as I only was about three miles from home. When we got to my apartment building, I invited him in for coffee and he accepted. We had sex in my bed and then he left."

James was quiet for a moment and then responded, "I have no doubt about what you have told me, but the problem is that none of Miamiville is in the City of Loveland. It is patrolled by Miami Township Police, Clermont County Sheriff and the Ohio Highway Patrol. Have to checked with them?" The male, in an agitated voice, said, "We went to Miami Township and they showed us the photos of their officers and Clermont County did the same. The officer was not in the photos."

James pushed the intercom and said, "Sally, bring in the photo album of our staff please." He set the book on the desk and the woman opened it up. She looked at each of the photos and then pointed to one and said simply, "Him."

James took a minute to compose his thoughts and said, "You are making a very serious allegation. Are you absolutely certain that this was the officer?" The male answered, "She is sure. What are you going to do?" James answered. "We will immediately conduct an investigation and take action as soon as it is completed. I hope she understands that she may have to give sworn testimony at an administrative hearing or criminal trial." The man said, "She will testify against him, I promise."

James got up out of his chair and said, "This will take a few days. You will be contacted by a detective who will get a written statement and we will let you know as soon as we complete the investigation. Thank you for coming to us and reporting this." James walked the couple to the exit then turned to Sally and asked. "Is Officer Andress on duty?" Sally nodded her head and said, "He is on shift for another two hours." James said, "Catch him before he leaves and have him report to my office."

Officer Bill Andress was a seven year veteran of the police department. He was thirty-one years old and married with a two year old son and a pregnant wife. Before joining Loveland, he had been a police officer for two years with another agency.

The door opened and Officer Andress walked in. James pointed to a chair and the officer immediately sat down. In a slow and measured voice James said, "I just received a complaint from a woman who says she had sex with you in her apartment after her car broke down. I do not want you to say anything at this point. You should get in contact with your union rep and get a lawyer before you make any statement. You are suspended with pay pending the outcome of the investigation. I need your badge and your gun."

Andress got out of the chair and removed the badge from his shirt and unholstered his gun, laying both on the desk. James pushed the intercom and told Sally to have the shift Sergeant come to his office. Moments later the office door opened and James told the Sergeant to escort the officer out of the building.

The door closed behind them and James stared at the badge and the gun on his desk. He had never suspended a cop before and his emotions were running wild, hoping that the allegations were not true. He picked up the gun and badge and placed them in the bottom drawer of his desk.

The door flew open and the Sergeant said, "Chief, you need to come to the parking lot. We have a situation." James jumped out of his chair and followed the Sergeant to the employee entrance. When he got to the parking lot, James saw a man slumped over the wheel of a car and blood spattered on the window. James ran over and saw Officer Andress' dead body in the driver's seat. James could tell that the officer was dead immediately. James looked at the Sergeant and said, "Go get the detective and have him bring a camera. Then call the coroner on the phone and have them come out here. I do not want this out over the radio. Let's keep this out of the news for as long as possible."

James stood outside of the officer's car and waited for the detective to arrive. He told the detective to get photos from all sides of the car and that they needed to recover the gun that was used. They found the semi-auto handgun on the floor in between the front seats. It was still cocked and had a bullet in the chamber.

It took about forty minutes for the Sheriff's pickup truck to arrive with two prisoners to pick up the body. The inmates pulled out a black body bag where they carefully placed the body. James told the Sergeant to call a wrecker using the telephone and to have them take the car to the Coroner's Lab as evidence.

James stood and watched as the wrecker picked up the car and then returned to the station. He walked into his office followed by the Sergeant who said, "Boss, Bill asked me to let him go to his locker because wearing the police belt without a gun looked stupid. I waited in the hallway to give him some privacy. I walked him to the door and watched him get into his car and then turned to come back in. That is when I heard the shot. I ran to the car and saw that he was clearly dead and that is when I came and got you."

James grabbed his car keys and walked to Sally to get the officer's home address. His home was a twenty minute drive and James spent every second of the trip trying to find the right words to tell a young wife that her husband had committed suicide. He also grappled with telling her that her husband had been suspended and the reason for the suspension.

***

James rang the doorbell of the home and a pregnant woman holding her little boy in her arms answered. She had a big smile on her face as she said, "Bill has not gotten home yet, but you are welcome to come in and wait for him Chief." The woman turned and walked toward the rear of the house and James followed behind. When the two arrived in the family room James said, "I am not here to see your husband, please have a seat." The young woman looked confused and sat down on the sofa. James sat in a chair across from her and said, "A little less than an hour ago your husband took his own life in his car in the parking lot of the police station. I am so sorry for your loss." The woman's voice shook in fear as she asked, "Why?" James answered, "I had just told Bill that needed his badge and gun and that he was suspended with pay pending an internal investigation that he had sex with a female whose car broke down. He apparently retrieved another gun from the locker and shot himself in his car."

The young wife began sobbing uncontrollably. James said, "You need to have someone with you, is there someone I can call to come stay with you?" The young wife gave James the phone number of her mother and James called, telling her that her daughter needed her and that he would stay with her daughter until she arrived.

James put the two year old on the carpet and played with the child while his mother was on the couch screaming and crying. It took about thirty minutes for her mother to arrive and James kept the two year old occupied. When James heard the front door open, he grabbed his hat and walked past the mother closing the front door behind him. Not a word was spoken between the two.

James got into his car and decided to call it a day and just drive home. He needed to hug his wife and vent.

***

The next morning James called a department meeting of all police staff. He arranged with the Miami Township Police to cover any calls for service so that the whole staff would be together.

James told the staff that the officer had been notified that he was being suspended and that the officer committed suicide in his vehicle in the parking lot. He told them that, based on the circumstances, officers attending the funeral service would not be authorized to use any city vehicles, but that were could wear their police uniform to the service. He told them that any officer scheduled to work during the time of the funeral could use vacation time to attend and that someone would cover their shift while they were gone. Two officers from first shift announced that they would be going to the service. James told the Sergeant to hold over one officer from the night shift for one officer and that he would cover the other officer's beat.

***

James dressed for work, this time wearing his bullet proof vest and a full gun belt. He parked his car in the lot and went inside to get a set of keys to a marked patrol unit. He drove to the southern end of the city and patrolled the subdivisions like he would expect any other cop to do. The radio cracked and sent him to a car crash on Lebanon Road with injuries. James activated the lights and siren and arrived at the crash site within two minutes. The crash involved two vehicles that collided head-on. The driver of the vehicle that crossed the center line was dead. The other driver had life-threatening head injuries. James requested a medical helicopter to the scene. Two Miami Township Police units arrived and shut down one end of the road. Clermont County Sheriff's car shut down the other end to give the chopper a place to land. Two Ohio Highway Patrol cars arrived and the State Police Sergeant walked up to James and asked, "Chief, how many car crash investigations have you done in the past fifteen or so years? Let us handle this one for you." James simply nodded his head and the Sergeant opened the trunk of his car and pulled out the equipment they would need to investigate the crash. Almost an hour later, the officer that James was covering for arrived and took his place. James was able to return to his real job as Chief of Police.

# CHAPTER EIGHTEEN

James made a call to the Civil Service Commission to schedule a written examination to fill the vacancy. He was told that a list of candidates would be created and that he would be required to pick one of the top three on the list.

An advertisement of the test date ran in the Cincinnati Enquirer newspaper and the Civil Service Commission told James that there were over two hundred applicants after just three days and that over fifty of those were working Cincinnati Police officers.

The written portion of the testing was done at Loveland High School in the cafeteria and the final number was two hundred and eighty-two applicants to fill one position. Two hundred and forty-one passed the written portion and moved on to the physical agility. The number pared to one hundred and thirty who moved on to the polygraph. The physical examination reduced the number to sixty-one.

The final list, which would be in effect for two years, was fifty-seven. Two of the top three applicants were Cincinnati Police and the third was a criminal justice major in college who would need to be sent to the Police Academy. James interviewed the top three and chose the Cincinnati cop who happened to be female. She would start three weeks after her hire date to allow her to close her time in Cincinnati.

***

James found that he was spending most of his work time in meetings. Because Loveland sits in three different counties, he was expected to attend the Chiefs Association monthly meetings in each of the counties. He also had to deal with three different jails and Court Clerks, who each had their own rules and requirements. This was an area which James felt took away from the effectiveness of the police department.

Now that the department was back to full staffing, James was able to imbed a full time officer in the regional drug abuse task force and get two officers assigned to the on-call Countywide SWAT and dive teams. His contact with the citizen mandate also was presenting issues which the community faced and the officers were actually buying into the program.

***

James went to bed early after an evening of watching television with his wife. He was soundly sleeping when the phone rang at three in the morning. He was groggy as the voice on the other end said, "Chief, one of our officers was shot and is in route to the hospital." James sprung out of the bed and asked, "What happened?" The Sergeant said, "We received a call of a domestic and when we responded, the ex-husband fired a single blast hitting Sergeant Amby in the chest. We returned fire and hit the suspect five times. He was transported to the hospital by life squad under guard. I have not received any information on the condition of either."

James told the Sergeant to remain at the scene until he could get the Lieutenant there and that he would be going to the hospital to get a report on the shot officer.

When James arrived at University Medical Center, the entrance was blocked off by Hospital Police. He activated the lights of his unmarked car and the hospital vehicle moved to let him pass. He parked in the driveway and entered the main lobby where he saw university cops, sheriff's deputies and city cops. James did not take the time to put on a uniform, so he had his badge hanging from a lanyard around his neck. The group of cops saw his badge and told him that his officer was taken to surgery on the fifth floor.

After about an hour of sitting in the waiting room, a surgical nurse came out and told James. Your officer suffered serious wounds from the buckshot that hit his stomach. Each piece of buckshot had to be removed individually and then the area around it cleaned and sanitized. He will be in surgery for several hours, but he appears to be strong and should recover after a period of time. You are welcome to wait, but there is nothing to be accomplished here. We will contact you when he gets through this portion. Have you had contact with his wife?" James answered, "She is being brought here in a police car and should arrive shortly. I will stay until she is briefed." The nurse said, "We will provide her sleeping quarters so she can be nearby."

James called Lt. Deacon to get an update from the scene. She told him that the Sheriff's Department had sent investigators and that the crime scene was quite large, but that they had completed processing it and would be leaving the area shortly. She told James that the suspect had been shot five times by officers and that he had just gotten out of surgery and was likely to survive. She said that the doctors told the officer guarding him that the suspect would remain at University Medical Center for several days and then would be moved to Drake Center, a long term rehabilitation center, for likely weeks before he could be transferred to the jail. James left after speaking to Amby's wife and giving her his cell phone number to call at any hour of the day or night.

James went home and got a few hours of sleep before stating his day in the office. He got a report from both the officer and the suspect's condition and then called the Clermont County Sheriff to coordinate a security detail for the suspect as he lacked the staff to provide a 24 hour a day guard. They worked out an arrangement to split the time for as long as it would take.

***

When Amby was moved to a hospital room, James made a trip to the hospital to let him know how much he was missed by the department. Amby smiled meekly and said, "Boss, remind me to never volunteer for overtime again." In talking to the surgeon, James learned that it would be highly unlikely that Amby would ever be able to return to duty as a police officer, but James never relayed that to the officer. James told Amby that he would receive full pay for as long as it took to recover and that his family would be taken care of by the department.

# CHAPTER NINETEEN

James was in his office working on the schedule when a call went out over the air of a silent robbery alarm at a small bank in the business district. He listened as the first two cars arrived at the location, and then heard one officer request the detective and the Chief respond.

James grabbed his hat and went out the door to his car, activating the lights and siren. When he arrived, he saw the parking lot encircled in crime scene tape. An officer approached and told him, "Chief, you need to know that this is a bloodbath." James carefully entered the bank and immediately saw the dead body of a female who appeared to be in her fifties. When he entered the caged area, he saw two more females, one in her thirties and the other in her sixties, laying dead on the floor from gunshot wounds.

James motioned for the officers inside the bank to follow him outside and, once out of the building, called the Ohio Bureau of Criminal Investigation and Identification in Columbus, Ohio to respond and help. BCI is a division of the Attorney General and is responsible for investigations and the state crime lab. James was told it would take about two hours to get a team from Columbus south to Loveland and they would be there. Just less than an hour later, a black BCI van with a regional investigator arrived at the scene and told James that two state vans and three forensic techs would be arriving shortly.

James watched in awe as the techs moved methodically about the scene. One was photographing every inch of the bank while another was collecting fingerprints. They notified the Clermont County Coroner who ordered that the bodies be transported to the Hamilton County Corner because they were a larger agency and better equipped to handle this type of crime.

All four local television stations arrived with live trucks and James decided that the hounds were not going to leave. He set up an area a block away. There were group of microphones set up and James approached the microphones to provide as much information as he felt he could without compromising the ongoing investigation. He said, "My name is James Daniels and I am the Police Chief of the City of Loveland. I will provide you as much information as I can without compromising the investigation which, obviously, is in a very early stage. I will not be taking any questions from the media at this time. At approximately nine-fifteen this morning, officers were dispatched to a silent robbery alarm at the Key Bank. On arrival, they found three victims deceased inside the bank. The investigation has been turned over to the Ohio Bureau of Criminal Investigation and they are currently processing the scene. We will meet with you again later in the afternoon to provide an update. Thank you for your patience." He immediately walked away with the hounds screaming questions which he ignored.

James ordered his two detectives to remain at the scene for the sole purpose of being gophers for the state team at the scene. He told the two men that they were to go for coffee or a food run, whatever the state people needed.

He ordered the streets around the bank closed off while the investigators were processing the scene.

The state investigator came over and told James, "As soon as we are done collecting the physical evidence we find, a tech will drive it to the crime lab. Someone attempted to corrupt the video from the bank, but we have a magician who specializes in recovering video that is damaged. Hopefully we will be able to get information on the suspects. We have recovered seventeen sets of fingerprints and would like to get people who did business in the bank yesterday afternoon or this morning to provide with a set of elimination prints. James made that announcement in the afternoon press briefing and the response was immediate with people showing up at the bank to be fingerprinted. That left only two sets that were unidentified. BCI would put them into the Automated Fingerprint Identification System, known as AFIS, to see if they were in the system.

James sent a detective to every business that had a view of the bank to see if they had any useful video. A clothing store had video of a car in the parking lot which was gone when officers first arrived. When the video was enhanced, it showed an Ohio license plate and the officers were able to run that plate providing an address. A search warrant was obtained and the S.W.A.T. team executed the warrant, finding no one at the home. Nothing of any value was found at the residence.

AFIS scored hits on both of the set of fingerprints and arrest warrants were obtained for all three suspects, the third being the owner of the vehicle. A search of the second suspect's apartment revealed a 9mm Glock handgun that, by smell, had been recently fired. The third suspect was not at home when officers arrived. A national alert via the police computer was broadcast for the vehicle and the suspects. Two days later, Loveland received a phone call from the Davie, Florida Police Department telling them they had the vehicle and the suspects in their custody. James ordered two detectives to get a flight into Miami and contacted the Fugitive Unit of the Clermont County Sheriff to pick them up. The Fugitive Squad sent three deputies in a marked Sheriff van to Davie to drive the suspects back to Cincinnati.

The Loveland detectives attempted to interview each of the suspects, who had been provided a lawyer by the Florida courts. The suspects were told not to make any statements to the police until they were provided legal counsel in Ohio. The suspects waived an extradition hearing in Dade County, Florida are were ordered to be returned to Ohio.

The suspects were each wrapped in a shock belt, which delivers ninety thousand volt charges when activated by remote control. They were told that they would get one bathroom stop and one meal on the fifteen hour drive north, so they needed to go to the bathroom before leaving.

The van pulled into a McDonald's in Dalton, Georgia and the suspects were given a Big Mac, fries and a Coke. Handcuffs were not necessary as the belt provided the necessary deterrence to any stupid act. They got a bathroom stop in Knoxville, Tennessee when the van made a stop for gas. The suspects were taken to the bathroom one at a time and the shock belt was removed so they could drop their pants. Two deputies escorted one suspect at a time.

The Loveland detectives flew home and were waiting for the suspects to arrive at the Clermont County Jail. A judge was arranged to go to the jail and order lawyers be appointed for each suspect.

The suspects continued to invoke their right to remain silent, so a prosecutor from Clermont County was brought into the interviews. The prosecutor told each suspect that he intended to seek the death penalty for the murders, but would take it off the table for the first one to provide information.

They continued to refuse to cooperate, so the investigators went back to solidifying the evidence needed to get convictions. Weeks went by and the first case was upcoming when the investigators received a call from the prosecutor that one of the three wanted to make a deal. They rushed to the jail where the suspect told them he was the driver of the getaway car and was not a participant in the killing of the people. He told them where the cash that was taken was hidden and who was actually carrying the gun that was used. In exchange for his testimony against the other two defendants, the death penalty was taken off the table.

James put a letter of commendation into the personnel files of the two detectives for their efforts in obtaining convictions. Both defendants were sentenced to death in the case.

# CHAPTER TWENTY

Over the next three months James was in constant contact with Sgt. Amby and his family. He was in the office when he received a call from a doctor treating Amby that told him the officer would never be able to return to law enforcement. The surgeries and rehabilitation had given the officer much of his mobility, but not enough to return to work. The doctor told James that he would be filing the appropriate documentation to get Amby a medical disability.

With that information, James contacted the Civil Service Commission to schedule a written promotion examination. Unlike the hiring process where any of the top three can be chosen, James would be required to promote the top scorer. The process became complicated when the high scorer on the examination was also the canine handler. James called him into the office and explained that he had a choice to make. James explained that the department was not large enough to support a supervisor whose primary position would be as a canine officer. Accepting the promotion would require that the dog be trained with a new handler because the city would not retire the dog for the handler to keep. The handler asked for time to talk to his wife before making a decision and James said he was good with that. Three days later the handler declined the promotion saying it was a family decision.

The officer who finished second was a female with eight years on the department and she accepted the position.

James then went to the other three sergeants to see who was interested in the detective supervisor position. When that was filled, he asked the remaining two sergeants to pick the shift they wanted based upon seniority. The female was assigned to the afternoon shift and sent to the state training academy for a two week police supervisor school.

***

The eligibility list for police officer was still valid so James called the second name to offer him the position. The Cincinnati cop said he changed his mind and was no longer interested. James contacted the next name who was a college student and would need to be sent to a police academy.  The new recruit would not be ready for patrol for nine months and scheduling the overtime was going to be a nightmare.

When he accepted the position, James called the Cincinnati Police Academy to see when their next police recruit class would begin. He was told that it would start in less than two weeks, so James would have to move quickly to make it work. He needed to get the approval of the City Council Law and Safety Committee for the ten thousand dollar tuition for the academy, which did not include the salary and benefits of the officer. Then he had to get the new officer sworn in as the Cincinnati academy required the officer to be both sworn and employed. Next was getting the officer all of the equipment he would need. After working feverishly, James worked out all of the kinks and the young man started his voyage into a new career.

James would receive weekly updates from the academy on the progress of his recruit and was happy that the young man was fitting in well with his class.

The police academy was almost half done when James received a call from the secretary of the academy telling him he needed to come to the academy to resolve an imminent problem. James jumped into his car and drove downtown. When he walked into the Academy, James was immediately escorted into the Commander's office. The Commander pointed to a chair and James sat down. The Commander said, "Chief, we received a complaint from a male Cincinnati police officer recruit alleging that your officer made sexual advances toward him. The Cincinnati Police sexual harassment policy is clear and succinct and we will be expelling your officer from the class. I wanted you to be here when I took the action in deference to you.

The recruit was called into the office and the Commander informed him of the expulsion. James looked at the young man, who appeared to be ready to cry, and told him that he needed to report to the Loveland Police Department at nine in the morning and to bring with him all of the equipment issued to him. James left the academy and returned to his office.

James contacted the Civil Service Commission to obtain the next three candidates. The first would also need to attend the police academy and James passed his name and moved onto the second, who was a police officer at Xavier University.

She accepted the position and was given a starting date.

## CHAPTER TWENTY-ONE

James was on his way back to the office from lunch at home when he heard a radio call of a suspicious man at a package handling store that he was just passing. He turned the car around and pulled into the driveway. He saw a male standing in front of the store and approached him trying to engage in conversation. The man reached his right hand behind his back and James reactively drew his gun, ordering the man to show his hands. The man made no attempt to move despite repeatedly being ordered to show his hands. Two cruisers whipped into the driveway and jumped out of their cars with their guns drawn. One officer approached the man and retrieved a .380 semi-automatic handgun from the man's back. Once the man was in cuffs, James holstered his gun and drove back to the station.

James was sitting at his desk when one of the officers walked in and said, "Boss, you scored a whale. The guy we popped is on the FBI Ten Most Wanted List and is wanted for bombing multiple abortion clinics around the country. The U.S. Marshals are on their way to gobble him up. I cannot see any reason for us to charge him with the gun since the Feds are going to swallow him up." James nodded his head and said, "I agree. Give the Marshals the weapon and that will enhance the sentencing in their case.

The rest of the day was uneventful. The next morning Sally walked into the office and said, "Chief, there is a film crew from *Inside Edition* in the lobby asking to interview you.

What do you want me to tell them?" James grabbed his hat and walked out to the lobby where he spent twenty minutes being interviewed about catching an abortion clinic bomber. That interview aired nationally that evening.

***

Things were running smoothly at the Police Department and James convinced his wife to take a train ride. They decided to take a little road trip to an old favorite train watching town and do a little antique shopping on the way. At a rest stop just south of Findlay, Ohio, they noticed a man dressed in a heavy black, long sleeved tactical shirt and pants with a saggy backpack. He got out of a car and walked behind the restroom building and disappeared. Considering the apparel and suspicious demeanor and the ninety degree temperature, they tried to keep an eye on him but he vanished. James called the state highway patrol to come and check on the man. Troopers entered the woods and they waited and watched until the troopers came out of the wooded area with the man in handcuffs. A Sergeant said they located the man in the woods armed with a .45 caliber handgun and one bullet. He planned to take his own life. The man told officers that he had driven more than one hundred and fifty miles to kill himself. The man was transported to a hospital and put on a mental hold. When the two got to Deshler, Ohio, the timing was perfect as they got a front row seat to watch CSX's locomotive that honors police, "Spirit of Law Enforcement" unexpectedly go through. The trip was both memorable and relaxing.

The fall turned into winter and the spring and things at the police department were running effortlessly. James received a call from the City Manager telling him that the city had decided to hold an event in the park to celebrate Independence Day ending in a firework display and James needed to develop a security plan. James detailed four uniformed officers to work the event and borrowed two four wheel ATVs for the officers to use.

After the show was over and the eleven o'clock closing time was approaching, the two teams of officers began clearing the park when they heard gunshots ring out at the other end of the park. The officers raced toward the sound of the gunfire and found five people shot. One was dead and two others had life threatening injuries. One of those two died in route to the hospital. The other two had non-threatening injuries and were also transported to the hospital. The officers called for help and police agencies from around the region responded. James also responded to the scene and ordered the park closed and declared a crime scene also closing all of the roads surrounding it to protect the integrity of the scene until daylight. The initial investigation determined that the two dead males had been shooting at each other after a verbal altercation and the other victims were just innocent bystanders.

The Safety Director called James and told him that City Council wanted a written report of the incident and James provided a twenty-seven page detailed report that took him three days to complete. The local media and residents were up in arms that this could happen and demanded action be taken to assure that it never happens again.

James was ordered to appear at an open council meeting to answer questions about what occurred. He told a packed chamber that, "Any strong police presence would result in screams of RACISM. The two shooters did not likely retrieve their guns from a locker, they brought them from home. Yet their parents either did not know, or did not care that they were armed. The fix to the problem is for parents, members of the clergy and concerned adults should be present at these events to monitor the activity of the children. His remarks were booed by the audience to which he responded, "The police are not the parents of these children and we cannot discipline them."

***

As the months passed, James loved going to work every day. He had a great staff and a supportive administration that gave him the latitude to serve the citizens of Loveland.

James was out on the golf course on a bright and sunny Sunday when the cell phone in the golf card started ringing. He answered and the shift sergeant said, "Chief, we just had an officer involved shooting on Loveland-Madeira Road about one mile from the station. This started as a simple traffic stop and the suspect is dead. The officer is uninjured. What do you want us to do?" James thought for a moment and said, "Secure the scene and do not touch anything. Close all of the surrounding streets. I will call the Cincinnati Force Investigation Team to respond and handle the investigation. Call the detective and have him go to the scene and photograph everything, but not touch anything. Isolate the officer and drive him back to the station. When you get there, take his weapon for evidence and immediately give him one of our spares. Advise him to contact the union or an attorney and to not answer any questions until he has representation. Contact the Lieutenant and have her respond to the scene. I will come to the station."

James called Cincinnati Police Communications and said, this is James Daniels, Police Chief of Loveland, I need you to call the Chief and tell him that I am requesting the FIT to investigate an officer involved shooting. The officer is at our PD and the scene has been secured pending their arrival." Cincinnati sent two members of the team to the scene and the other two went to interview the officer.

James left the country club and drove directly to the Police Department. When he arrived, the officer was seated at a table with his hands over his face crying. James poured the cop a cup of coffee and said, "I am not going to ask you any questions because the Cincinnati Police will be investigating what happened. You have the right to wait seventy-two hours to make a statement and I would suggest that you utilize that option."

The investigators at the scene found a recently fired 9mm handgun near the body of the dead male. A search of the suspect's car revealed a cache of already packaged drugs and money in a duffle bag in the back seat.

Two investigators arrived at the station and sat down to interview the officer. They told him he had the right to have a union representative and/or an attorney present with him. The officer told them he had contacted the union and they were sending an attorney. The interview was terminated until the lawyer arrived.

Everyone left the room so the officer could talk privately with his attorney. The attorney walked out of the room and told everyone that his client would provide a written statement within the seventy-two hour window and they left the station together.

As word spread that a black man had been killed by a cop, protestors began arriving outside of the police department. James put out a call for assistance and units from Clermont, Hamilton and Warren County Sheriff's office, along with the Ohio Highway Patrol and Blue Ash, Mason, Miami Township, Milford, Montgomery and Union Township Police Departments all sent cars to assist. They established a staging area in the parking lot of Loveland High School and donned riot gear to prepare for any potential violence.

James put out a notice that there would be a press conference in front of the police department and had a lectern placed outside the main entrance to the police department. When he walked out to the lectern, there were microphones from the local media attached. James announced, "Early this afternoon we had an officer involved shooting of an African-American male on Loveland-Madeira Road. That case is being investigated by the Cincinnati Police Force Investigation Team and the results of their investigation will be turned over to the Hamilton County Prosecutor. We will not be releasing any information as to the identities of the people involved. That will come from the Prosecutor. I will not be taking any questions." He turned around and walked back into the station,

Over the next two hours, the number of protestors grew to over one hundred, many of whom were carrying signs declaring cops as 'murderers' and 'killers'. When the crowd began to block the driveway of the fire department. James ordered the more than fifty police vehicles out of the staging area to positions around the roadways around the police department. He sent four of his officers to move the crowd from the fire driveway and had the other officers suit up in riot gear. The crowd moved from the entrance, only to sit down in the center of the four lane Loveland-Madeira Road shutting down the flow of traffic. With a line of riot-equipped cops behind him, James walked into the street and ordered the protestors to move immediately or face arrest. The Hamilton County Sheriff had sent a prisoner bus which was moved into the full view of the protestors.

The protestors ignored the order and James announced, "You have five minutes to move from the street. Everyone still blocking the street will be arrested." He made the group aware of the time left until the five minutes expired. A few of the people moved from the street and, when the clock ran out, James motioned for officers to move in and start making arrests. One woman punched an officer and was immediately was taken to the ground and subdued. She was bleeding from her nose and was taken to the hospital by the life squad with a cop riding with her. The prisoners were loaded into the prisoner bus and taken to the Hamilton County Jail. They were all charged with misdemeanor Obstructing Official Business. The remainder of the protestors left the area.

***

The next morning James was at the Hamilton County Municipal Court for the arraignment of the people arrested. The judge announced, "I will be handling all of the cases from the protest yesterday in succession. All those who plead not guilty will be given a bond of ten thousand dollars at ten percent. Those who plead no contest or guilty will be given a fine of one hundred dollars plus court costs. This applies to all of the defendants except for the one charged with resisting arrest and felony assault on a police officer."

Ten of the thirty-two plead no contest and the others were given a trial date and released after posting the one thousand dollar bail.

James was the only witness to testify at each of the trials and all were found guilty.

***

James made it a point to attend all Council meetings whether or not the police department had items on the agenda. He wanted to be available if a resident had a question or issue. The meeting was almost over when a black female walked up to the microphone and demanded that the council purchase and mandate the cops wear body worn cameras. She railed on the cases of Travon Martin, Ahmed Aubrey and yelled those cops need to be held accountable for the murder of black males.

The mayor looked at James for a response. In a measured tone, James looked directly at the woman and said, "Let me begin with your reference to specific cases. George Zimmerman is not, nor was he ever a police officer. He was charged and found not guilty by a jury which did not have a single police officer sitting on it. The man who shot Mister Aubrey is not, nor was he ever, a police officer. His father retired as an investigator for the District Attorney, but the shooting had nothing to do with law enforcement. Three men in that case have been charged with Murder and a jury of non-cops will determine their fate."

"Now, let me address the wearing of cameras. A video is a true and accurate depiction of exactly and only what the lens sees. It is not necessarily a true and accurate depiction of the event. Think of an NFL football game. The quarterback throws a pass to the sideline which is caught by the receiver. The official standing less than ten feet away rules the receiver only got one foot inbounds, making it an incomplete pass. The network television will show the play from seven different camera views of the same play. Four of them are inconclusive, two others appear to show the receiver's right foot did not touch inbounds. The last camera view, when run in slow-motion, shows the right foot of the receiver move two blades of grass before stepping out of bounds. The call is reversed. Were the other six cameras wrong? I am strongly opposed to the purchase, actually the waste of money, for body worn cameras."

One councilman immediately made a motion that the city purchase body worn cameras for all officers. The motion died for lack of a second. The woman stormed out of the council chamber and the meeting ended.

## CHAPTER TWENTY TWO

James and his wife were putting the dinner dishes away when she announced, “I am going to put my retirement papers in this week. I think thirty-six years at P&G is enough. I will fill my time at the club playing tennis and maybe even take golf lessons.”

James just laughed and answered, “You have more than paid your dues. You could even go spend time with our kids. I, on the other hand, am loving what I do too much to walk away. The minute it quits being fun, I will leave in a New York minute.”

James went into the office and started looking for a cruise to celebrate her retirement.

He found a seven day cruise that originated in Seattle, Washington and went to Juneau, Alaska. He was in the process of registering for the trip when the intercom announced, “Chief, U.S. Secret Service is here to see you.” She brought the two agents into the office and they told James that the President of the United States would be doing a town hall meeting at the Oasis Golf and Conference Center and that they needed to get the security arrangements arranged. Loveland Police would need to provide security at the venue and close down the streets the motorcade would be travelling to get to and from the Cincinnati airport, which is in Kentucky. He would only have six days to get it ready.

The motorcade would travel north on Interstate 75 into Cincinnati and then north on Interstate 71 to Interstate 275. It would have a Cincinnati Police and Hamilton County Sheriff escort. Secret Service would have two routes to get to the Conference Center and would not announce which route until the Air Force One was on the ground meaning that the street closures would be last minute.

James waited until the agents left his office and then made the cruise registration. He immediately went to work getting a plan together to keep the President safe.

James contacted all of the regional law enforcement agencies to set up a meeting and invited a representative from Secret Service. They divided the intersections and interstate onramps that would need to be closed off and the perimeter security for the event. James told Secret Service that they would have responsibility for the venue security.

The morning of the event, Secret Service offered James the opportunity to ride in the technology van in the motorcade. James drove to downtown Cincinnati and got into the van, which he learned had communication capability with every police frequency in Greater Cincinnati. The operator was able to notify agencies of the route as it progressed and the thirty mile drive ran smoothly.

James had four uniformed officers in marked cruisers around the exterior of the Conference Center and Secret Service had two agents at the front entrance screening everyone with a metal detector. They also had an agent on the rear entrance and one more covering the kitchen entrance. Two agents were assigned to the crowd of invited guests numbering about three hundred people. James wore a suit to be inside and the agents made sure that he got to personally meet the President.

After the event was over, James returned to his office and immediately issued an invoice to the White House for thirty-nine thousand dollars to recover the costs his city incurred. He never received a response.

***

James closed out the last work day before leaving for his celebration cruise. The last thing he did was put his gun and city issued phone in his desk. He did not feel the need for either.

James and Karen drove the Cincinnati Northern Kentucky International Airport and parked in the Airport Police parking lot with their permission. A police cruiser took the two to the terminal and they boarded the jet for Seattle. The five hour flight was uneventful, but the two were tired from sitting in their seats. It was chilly and raining in Seattle when they arrived.

They grabbed a taxi to their hotel and checked in for the night. They went to the front desk and James asked the desk clerk for recommendations on places to enjoy a dinner. The clerk smiled and said, "I don't recommend our guests leave the hotel after dark because of the violence occurring in our downtown streets. Our restaurant has high quality food and it is safer than walking the downtown.

After dinner was over, they went up to their room which had a spectacular view over the downtown area. James stood and looked out the window seeing flashing police lights and cops in riot gear apparently facing off with a group in the center of a four lane street. He could not hear anything that was said between the cops and the protestors, but he watched as the cops threw flash-bangs into the crowd. The crowd did not disperse and the cops did not make any moves toward the group. James could see additional police cars arriving, but did not understand why they made no effort to disperse the crowd other than now firing tear gas. James grabbed a chair and sat and watched the standoff that lasted over an hour with no visible arrests or attempts to move toward the crowd. The street was shut down to vehicular traffic the whole time. James now understood the concerns the desk clerk had.

The next morning, they boarded a cruise bus to be transported to the ship. The street in front of the hotel still had the litter from the night before. They boarded the ship and were taken to their stateroom which had an outside view for them to watch as they moved out into the ocean. There was a knock on the door of their room and a cruise staff member offered to give them a tour of the ship. She told them that there would be approximately twenty-five hundred people taking the cruise and that the meal times were staggered to accommodate all of the people. She took them up the elevator to the top level and showed them the large outdoor swimming pool and the bar with free drinks for the guests. She showed them the exercise room and the ballroom which featured live entertainment each evening.

She led them to the dining area which appeared to seat approximately one thousand people. They would be served three full meals and there was a menu which was available twenty-four hours. The main meals would be served buffet style and there were seven different bars for the guests.

The buffet was much more than they expected. There was prime rib, lobster, sea bass and Alaskan crab available. After dinner they went up to the top deck and sipped on brandy as they marveled at the sight of nothing but black in all directions. They went to bed and slept well. In the morning, they returned to the pool area and saw the expanse of the ocean like a blank canvas waiting to be painted. They ate breakfast with one thousand of their new friends and spent the day at the pool. After dinner, they went to listen to the music of a Beach Boys tribute band that had the crowd dancing in the aisles with the greatest hits of the band.

Day three brought them into Alaska and they could see the beauty of the land. Far off they could see snowcaps, even though it was the end of June. The evening brought a chill in the air and they had to return to their stateroom for warmer clothing.

They were having the time of their lives and loving every minute. They decided to order dinner in the room and it was delivered by a nice young man. After they finished dinner, Karen said she was not feeling well and needed to lay down. She got into the bed and immediately began vomiting uncontrollably. James grabbed the phone and asked for medical assistance, which arrived within minutes. The ship doctor and two nurses noticed that her lips were turning blue indicating a lack of oxygen. The doctor told James that this did not appear to be normal food poisoning and requested a medical helicopter to the ship. They took Karen to the heliport where the helicopter was waiting for them. On the way up, the doctor told James that security had closed off their room and it was being treated as a crime scene. He also said that their personal belongings would be delivered to the hospital within hours.

The helicopter had one surgeon and two emergency room nurses onboard. When they got her onto the chopper, the doctor did a medically induced coma to reduce the damage to her.

The helicopter landed at a Level One Trauma center in Juno, Alaska and a surgical team was on the heliport awaiting them. She was taken directly into surgery and a social worker escorted James to a waiting area. James called the twins and told each what had transpired and that he would keep them updated as soon as he knew more.

It was a little than two hours later that the surgeon came into the room and told James, "We did everything we possibly could to save your wife, but our efforts were unsuccessful. She was in no pain and passed peacefully." James slumped down falling into a chair in the waiting room with his hands covering his face sobbing uncontrollably. After a short period of time, he regained his composure knowing that this was neither the time or place to fall apart. The doctor continued, "This case is being treated as a homicide and the FBI is at the ship as we speak. Two agents from Anchorage are on the way here to talk to you. Your wife is being taken to the basement where an autopsy will be performed to determine cause of death. I am so sorry for your loss."

The social worker brought James a cup of coffee and told him, "I will remain with you until you leave here. If you want to talk, I am here for you. If you want quiet, I understand that as well."

Less than an hour later two men in suits walked into the room. Both pulled out cases showing their badge and identification. James pulled out his wallet showing them his badge and id also. The one agent said, "Chief, we already know who you are and will extend every professional courtesy we can. This is what is happening as we speak. There is a forensic team on the ship and they have taken the food and plates from your dinner. They will be airlifted to the FBI lab in D.C. for analysis. Agents are interviewing the people who prepared the food as well as the server who delivered it. There were two other people who became sick, but your wife is the only one who died. I will keep you updated as we get more information."

James told the agents that his wife wanted to be cremated and asked if that could be done here in Alaska. The agents said that they would have the body picked up by a funeral home and that the process might take a day or two.

The agents drove James to a downtown hotel and his luggage was already there. He went up to his room and stood at the window crying uncontrollably. When he finally got his composure, he called each of the twins and gave them the devastating news. He told them that he would be bringing their mother's body back to Cincinnati the next day. He laid down on the bed knowing that sleep was not going to be an option.

The front desk called him the next morning telling him that there was a man at the desk to speak to him. James went to the lobby and a man in a business suit walked up and told him, "I have the remains of your wife." As he turned to return to his room, the two FBI agents who he had earlier contact with told him they were able to get him a direct flight to Cincinnati with a short layover in Minneapolis. They offered to drive him to the airport.

James was able to pay for a second seat for his wife's remains to travel. The trip was uneventful, but long. When he landed in Cincinnati, there were two airport cops waiting at the gate. They informed James that there were media cameras waiting in the public area because the death had been on the network news. If he chose not to speak to the media, they would cover him. His failure to respond answered their question and they whisked him past the media hounds and took him to a waiting police car. The officer in the cruiser helped him load his luggage and drove him the one-half mile to his car. As the cruiser passed the front entrance to the police department, James saw a line of cops standing at attention and saluting to honor his loss.

He drove slowly north to go home. When he pulled into his driveway, he felt a rush of emptiness walking into the house. He went directly to the cherry wood dining room table and carefully placed the urn in the middle. It was now the centerpiece of a table that had been used for holidays and special meals for well over thirty years. James moved into the family room and sat down in his favorite chair, placing his head into his hands and sobbing. In less than ten minutes, the front doorbell rang and the state trooper's widow was outside with a plate of food for him. She came into the house and told James, "You both were there for me when my husband passed, now I am here for you in your time of need. James told the woman he had no appetite, but she insisted he eat the home cooked meal she made for him. James was slowly eating when the whole neighborhood showed up at his door with food and desserts. They all said that they too felt the loss he was experiencing. The next group to show up were from the city and included the Mayor, City Manager, Safety Director, Fire Chief, Public Works Director and all of the members of the City Council. Loveland cops, both on and off duty came to tell James how sorry they were for his loss and offering to do anything for him that they could. Sally, the police clerk, came in and told James, "I took a comp day today and tomorrow. I came to help you make the arrangements and take phone calls and whatever else you need done."

James asked her to contact Saint Savior Church in Montgomery, Ohio to conduct the funeral mass and then contact the cemetery with the information.

It was late afternoon when his daughter, her husband and his granddaughter arrived. They had made the five hour drive up from Nashville and they all appeared to be worn out. James told them to take the master bedroom because it offered the space for the baby's crib. He did not tell them that he doubted that he would ever be able to sleep in that bed again.

The stream of people continued coming and going until well after dark. When the house finally emptied, James got a blanket and pillow and went to sleep on the couch in the family room.

The doorbell rang early the next morning and the trooper's widow was there with breakfast for the family. She made a large omelet, potatoes and a thermos filled with coffee for the family to sit and enjoy. They all ate at the dining room table, looking directly at the urn. Sally arrived as they were finishing and told them that the mass would be in two days and the interment would immediately follow. She said the police department was receiving calls from agencies from throughout the region asking how they could participate. She told them a request had been made for the Cincinnati Police Honor Guard to escort the urn, but they had to decline because it was not a line of duty death.

Kelly went to the Cincinnati airport to pick up Dennis and his partner and bring them to the house. There were lots of tears shed as the family tried to deal with the loss of Karen.

## CHAPTER TWENTY-THREE

James had been informed that the city was providing an officer and a patrol vehicle to transport the urn to the church and then to the gravesite.

The officer, in his dress uniform and wearing white gloves, arrived at the door to lead them to the church. When they arrived at the church, the parking lot was already full. There were marked police cars from multiple agencies in the lot.

There were two lines of cops in uniform standing at attention and saluting on the sidewalk leading to the church entrance. As the officer passed carrying the urn, two officers would drop the salute as the urn passed and it was done with precision as if they had practiced it many times.

Because there was no funeral home involved, the officer took the urn up to the front door and handed it over to the priest who was waiting at the door with two altar boys. The priest took the urn and walked down the center aisle of the church with James and the children following. James was astounded to see the pews completely full and the overflow lining the walls of the church. As he made his way to the first row, which had been reserved for them, he saw police officers wearing their uniforms, even though they were there on their own time.

The priest was at the lectern when he told the people attending, "I am sure James would like to make some comments." He motioned for James to come up. James slowly walked up the steps of the altar and to the lectern. His voice was breaking as he said, "We are here today to celebrate the life of my wife, the mother of my children and the best friend I will ever have. Whether you worked with her at P&G, knew her from the country club, or are a member of my extended family of law enforcement, my family thanks you for coming. There is a hole in my heart which will never be filled, but there is solace in the love being shown to my family here today. I will never be able to re-pay the debt of gratitude I owe all of you." With that, James walked down to the bottom of the altar steps and placed his fingers to his mouth. He then touched the urn giving his wife a final kiss.

The priest completed the service and carried the urn to the front door, giving it to the cop. James and the family were following immediately behind. The officer returned to his patrol car and James drove the priest and the altar boys in his car which was followed by the twins and their families.

It was a six mile ride from the church to the cemetery. As the short procession drove, it passed police, fire and EMS vehicles with their overhead lights silently flashing and the occupants standing at attention beside their vehicles saluting the procession. When they arrived at the gravesite, the officer handed the urn to the priest, then saluted and left.

The graveside service was short and the urn was placed inside of a crypt. The twins drove back to the house and James returned the priest and boys to the church. As

James drove back to his house, the enormity of the whole situation caught up with him and he wanted to be in that urn with his wife for eternity.

Kelly had to be back in Nashville for her work, so they left in the afternoon. Dennis and his partner had plane reservations for the next morning.

***

For the next two weeks James only left the house to go to the grocery store. Only the widow came to the house to check on him and bring him meals. James would get very depressed and the only thing that kept him functioning was that he would think about something that he and Karen had done together. Like the time they both cried at the end of watching the final episode of the television show *M.A.S.H.* or the time they both cheered when Rudy got put into the final football game of his senior year at Notre Dame in the movie *Rudy*.

After two weeks, James returned to the office in his Chief's uniform. He really did not know what to expect, but he was treated as if nothing was different. Dawn caught him up on the happenings over the period of his absence and everyone went about doing their jobs. Sally announced, "Chief, there is an FBI agent here who says he needs to talk to you."

The FBI agent came into the office and said, "Chief, I am assigned to the Cincinnati office and was sent out here to tell you that an arrest was made in the death of your wife. The nineteen year old suspect delivered the food you ate. He told investigators that he did not intend to kill anyone, he just wanted to make them sick so they would sue the cruise line. He was angry that he had been denied a promotion. He has been charged with Murder and will be tried in Federal Court in Seattle." James thanked him for the information and the agent left.

After just one week back at work, James knew that the only way that he would keep his sanity was to get far away from Loveland. He put in retirement papers with the State of Ohio, sold his country club membership and put his house up for sale. While the sales were all in process, James flew to Palm Beach, Florida to buy a beach front house on the ocean.

He rented a car at the airport and just drove aimlessly along the Atlantic Ocean to see what property might be available. When he was unable to locate anything interesting, he continued driving until he reached Fort Lauderdale, where he spent the night.

The next morning, he made a stop at Fort Lauderdale Police Department and asked about getting a referral for a real estate agent to help him. One of the cops told him that his brother in-law was an agent and called him to come to the station. The agent listened and told James that he knew of no residential properties on the beach for sale, but there was one property which had a perfect view of the ocean nearby. The agent took James to see the small three bedroom home which had a screened-in porch with a dynamic view of the Atlantic Ocean. The agent told James that the property was overpriced and that banks would not give loans to buy the one-half million dollar price tag.

After looking at the property, the two men went to a restaurant for coffee. James told the agent that paying cash was not an issue and to make an offer of four hundred thousand dollars to the owner. He left and returned to the airport to go home.

***

James returned to the office while awaiting the approval of the state retirement board. The sale of the club membership was completed and the house had received a good amount of interest. One of the things that the couple had taken care of was life insurance. They purchased individual policies in the amount of two million dollars. That, coupled with both of their pensions and his 401k from his bank employment, would leave him set for life.

James received a call from the real estate agent that the owner of the house in Florida accepted his offer, but suggested that James retain an attorney for the closing. James immediately contacted the Florida Bar Association and received three names of attorneys in that area who specialized in real estate law.

His last day of employment as the Police Chief was an emotional day for all. There were many hugs shared and the administration purchased a catered lunch for all to share. Handing his badge and gun to the Safety Director was one of the most difficult things James had ever done.

## CHAPTER TWENTY-FOUR

James hired a moving company to get the furnishings from Loveland, Ohio to Fort Lauderdale, Florida. He donated his bedroom set to a Catholic charity because he knew he would never be able to sleep in it alone.

His days in Florida were spent playing golf and sitting on the screen porch watching the ocean. He wrote an article on issues facing small police departments and submitted it to POLICE MAGAZINE, who published it and sent him a check for four hundred dollars. They offered him a position as a contributing writer to write about individual issues facing smaller agencies. He found something new that both filled his time and provided satisfaction.

As the years passed, he never stopped missing his wife, but the great years they shared together gave him memories that he was able to cherish. That brought him the solace and peace he so badly needed.

CPSIA information can be obtained
at www.ICGtesting.com
Printed in the USA
JSHW052154250522
26330JS00007B/255

9 781792 374722